The WORRY Website

Jacqueline Wilson

Illustrated by Nick Sharratt

Corgi Yearling Books

THE WORRY WEBSITE
A CORGI YEARLING BOOK : 978 0 440 86480 6 (from January 2007)
0 440 86480 1

First published in Great Britain by Doubleday,
an imprint of Random House Children's Books

Doubleday edition published 2002
Corgi Yearling edition published 2003

10

Copyright © Jacqueline Wilson, 2002
Lisa's Worry copyright © Lauren Roberts, 2002
Illustrations copyright © Nick Sharratt, 2002

The right of Jacqueline Wilson to be identified as the
author of this work has been asserted in accordance with
the Copyright, Designs and Patents Act 1988.

All rights reserved. No part of this publication may be reproduced,
stored in a retrieval system, or transmitted in any form or by any means,
electronic, mechanical, photocopying, recording or otherwise,
without the prior permission of the publishers.

Papers used by Random House Children's Books are natural,
recyclable products made from wood grown in sustainable forests.
The manufacturing processes conform to the environmental regulations of the country of origin.

Set in Palatino

Corgi Yearling Books are published by Random House Children's Books,
61–63 Uxbridge Road, London W5 5SA,
a division of The Random House Group Ltd,
in Australia by Random House Australia (Pty) Ltd,
20 Alfred Street, Milsons Point, Sydney, NSW 2061, Australia,
in New Zealand by Random House New Zealand Ltd,
18 Poland Road, Glenfield, Auckland 10, New Zealand,
and in South Africa by Random House (Pty) Ltd,
Isle of Houghton, Corner of Boundary Road & Carse O'Gowrie,
Houghton 2198, South Africa.

THE RANDOM HOUSE GROUP Limited Reg. No. 954009

www.**kidsatrandomhouse**.co.uk

A CIP catalogue record for this book is available from the British Library.

Printed and bound in Great Britain by
Cox & Wyman Ltd, Reading, Berkshire

To Katie, Rhiannon and Alice

HOLLY'S WORRY

Type in your worry:

OK.

I think I'm going to get a stepmother.

There are lots of stepmothers in my favourite book of fairy tales. Don't go, 'Yuck, boring!' Fairy tales are seriously cool, *much* scarier than any X-rated video you've ever secretly watched at a sleepover. Snow White's stepmother is the scariest of all.

She doesn't *look* scary. She looks beautiful in the picture in my book – though her long queen's robes are spoilt because Hannah tried to colour them with purple wax crayon. I was FURIOUS. I felt like snapping the book shut and smacking Hannah round the head with it, even though she's only little and didn't *mean* to spoil the picture.

I minded so because it's such a special book. It used to be our mum's when she was a little girl. She gave it to me. Snow White's mum died when she was born so she got this stepmother who looked so lovely that her magic mirror said she was fairest of them all. But she was evil and mean and dead jealous when the mirror said Snow White was the fairest now, so the stepmother tried to have her chopped into bits and then she poisoned her with an apple and she fell down dead and was kept in a glass coffin until a handsome prince came by (*yawn!*) and brought her back to life. The wicked stepmother was so maddened  that she boiled with rage and her shoes stayed so red hot she couldn't take them off and she had to dance until she died.

She must have had awful blisters. I've got one

where my old trainers are rubbing. Dad doesn't always get it together when we need new shoes. It's not his fault he's so busy. Yes it is. I'm not making excuses for my dad any more. I can't stick him now. And I especially can't stick *her*.

I'm going to add to my worry.

I wish she was wicked.

That sounds daft. Mr Speed will think I'm seriously weird. Mind you, Mr Speed is a little bit weird himself. He's speedy, like his name. He whizzes up and down the school corridors, he dodges round the desks in the classroom, and he skips across the playground. He really *did* skip once when Claire brought a skipping rope to school. He could do all sorts of fancy footwork too – but then he tripped and fell over and said a *very* rude word. He's not a bit like the other teachers.

This Worry Website is all his idea. It's instead of Circle Time. You know, when you all sit in a circle, fidgeting, and you're meant to discuss your problems. Sometimes it's dead boring because someone like Samantha bangs on about missing her dad. Everyone always feels sorry for Samantha because she's so little and pretty with lovely long fair hair. Even Mr Speed has a special smiley way of looking at her that makes me sick.

Sometimes Circle Time is terribly embarrassing because someone stupid like poor William confides the sort of problem that should stay a deadly secret. He told the whole class that he wets the bed and his dad yells at him and makes him cry and his mum says she can't keep up with washing his sopping sheets. Some of the kids giggled and poor William looked as if he was going to cry again. Mr Speed got *very* fierce with the gigglers and praised William for being so honest and sensible over a tiny physical problem that happens to heaps of people – but even Mr Speed couldn't stop half the class calling poor William 'Wetty Willie' in the playground.

So maybe that's why he came up with the Worry Website idea.

'I've designed the super-cool, wacky, wicked website on the classroom computer, OK? Any time any of you have a problem then access the Worry Website when it's your turn on the computer and type it in. You don't need to put your name. Then we can all contribute our comments and suggestions – make them *kind* and *constructive* or I'll leap up and down on you in my Doc Martens, get it?'

We got it.

Everyone started typing in their worries. Someone had a good long moan about their sneaky sister and their brainy brother.

Someone was worried about being bottom of the class.

Someone wrote about having scary nightmares.

Someone was sad because their pet rat had just died.

One of the boys wrote that he liked one of the girls a lot. That made everyone giggle – and Greg went very pink. Hmm! I wonder who he fancies?

Someone else went on and on. *Oh boo hoo, it's so sad, I miss my dad, etc, etc.* We all know who *that* was. At least Samantha can still see her dad when she goes to stay with him and his new girlfriend.

Well, I see my mum. Sometimes. I have to take my  little sister Hannah so she can get to know our mum. She left when Hannah was just a baby. Mum had Depression which made her very sad so she cried a lot and then ran off. When she ran off I guess Dad and Hannah and I got Depression too because we all felt very sad and cried a lot as well. It felt very scary when Dad cried so I told him that it was OK. *I'd* look after him and Hannah now.

I do look after both of them. I've been almost like

11

Hannah's mum. When she was a baby I fed her and washed her and dressed her and changed her (yucky, but you have to do it). I cuddled her lots and played peek-a-boo and do you know something? The very first word she said was Holly. That's my name.

She's said millions and millions and millions of words since. She is a total chatterbox. She's in the Reception class at my school and Miss Morgan obviously adores her – though she always gets into trouble for talking. She even talks during Story Time. She doesn't mean to be naughty. She just likes to join in.

I read to her at bedtime from my special book of fairy tales. She likes 'Red Riding Hood' best, especially the wolf bits. 'Oh, Grandma, what big teeth you've got,' I say in a teeny-tiny Red Riding Hood voice and then Hannah shrieks, 'All the better to EAT YOU ALL UP!' and bounces up out of bed at me, gnashing her teeth. Once she bit me on the nose by accident. She can be a very boisterous baby sister.

12

My favourite fairy tale is 'Snow White'. When I read the start of the story out loud and say that Snow White's hair is as black as coal and her skin as white as snow and her lips as red as berries, Hannah always shouts, '*Holly* berries!' and stabs at the picture with her finger.

'That's you, Holly,' she says.

I wish! I don't look the slightest bit like Snow White. I *have* got red lips (especially if I've been eating red Smarties) but I often have a red nose too (I get lots of colds). My hair is straggly mouse (though my *nails* are sometimes as black as coal). Snow White is as pretty as a picture. *Her* picture in the book is beautiful, with tiny glass mirrors and red apples all round the border and Snow White herself is wearing a white dress embroidered all over with tiny gold stars. Snow White is small too, not that much bigger than the Seven Dwarves, and she's thin as a pin. I am not pretty. I am as plain as an empty page and a bit on the podgy side too.

I don't care. I take after my dad. I used to be glad. I used to love my dad *sooooooo* much. Whenever he collects us from the After School Club he always

13

says, 'Where are my special girlfriends?' I have always been his Big Grown-up Girlfriend and Hannah his Teeny Tiny Girlfriend. But now Dad has a real girlfriend. I'm scared she's going to come and live with us and be my stepmother and it's not fair.

'Yes, it is so fair,' said Hannah. 'We *want* her to be our mother.'

'No, we've *got* a mother already. You remember, Hannah,' I said.

'Not really,' said Hannah.

We haven't gone on a visit to our mum for quite a while. We *want* to, but the last time we didn't get on with Mum's new boyfriend, Mike.

'Oh yes! He shouted and we cried,' said Hannah.

'You cried. I'm not a baby,' I said.

'You did so cry, I saw. I don't like that Mike. *Or* our mum,' said Hannah.

'Yes you do,' I insisted.

'No, I like our *new* mum much, much, much more,' said Hannah.

You will never guess who this new mum is going to be. Miss Morgan. Yes, *that* Miss Morgan. Hannah's teacher.

'I love her to bits,' said Hannah happily.

Dad loves her to bits too.

I suppose I used to like her just a little bit myself. I used to take Hannah into her classroom every

morning. Dad has to drop us off at school very early
or else he'll be late for work. Miss Morgan is always
there though. I used to like seeing what she
was wearing. She doesn't look a bit like a
teacher. She's got long hair way past her
shoulders and she wears long dresses
too, all bright and embroidered, and she
has these purple suede pointy boots with
high heels. She looks as if she's stepped
straight out of my fairy-story book.

I liked the way her Reception
classroom looked too. It was all so
bright and cosy and small. I'd hang about
for a while, keeping an eye on Hannah,
showing her the water trough and the giant
building bricks and the powder paints and the
playhouse. I especially loved the playhouse. I hadn't
had much time for playing since Hannah was born. I

suddenly wanted to scrunch
up small and squeeze in
through the tiny door and
squat safe inside, too little
to do anything else but
play.

I didn't, of course. I'm
not daft like poor William.
But Miss Morgan saw me

staring, and the next day when I dropped Hannah off she asked me if I'd be sweet enough to tidy up the dolls and the little beds and tables and chairs because all those four-year-olds had got them all higgledy-piggledy.

I sighed a bit, like I didn't really want to, and then I leant through the open window of the playhouse and sorted it all out. It was kind of fun. I don't know why. Doing it for real is no fun at all. Still, the playhouse dolls didn't whine or fidget or refuse to put their arms in their cardie like *someone* I could mention.

The next morning Miss Morgan said, 'Guess what, Holly, the playhouse is in a mess *again*.' I sighed and said, 'I suppose you want me to fix it?' – and so it got to be a habit. I also put fresh water in the trough and cleaned up the sandpit and tested out the building bricks to see if there were enough to make a proper fairy-tale palace like the pictures in my book. Hannah didn't join in these early morning games. She just wriggled onto Miss Morgan's lap and chattered to her non-stop.

'Feel free to tip her off your lap whenever you get tired. She does tend to go on and on,' I said.

Miss Morgan didn't seem to mind a bit. I sometimes wished I could climb on her lap and chatter too, just like Hannah. Miss Morgan used to be my favourite teacher in the school – even better than Mr Speed.

Dad met Mr Speed and Miss Morgan when he came to Parents' Evening. Dad said that Mr Speed was very pleased with my progress and that he said I was a very good, sensible girl and the little star of his class. I twinkled. Dad said that Miss Morgan was very pleased with Hannah too and that she said she was very lively and loving. If Miss Morgan had said Hannah was very good or sensible she would be a terrible fibber.

'Mr Speed's smashing, isn't he, Dad?' I said happily.

'Yes he is,' said Dad. 'Miss Morgan's rather special too, isn't she?'

Dad took to coming into Hannah's class with us every morning even though it made him late for work. Then Miss Morgan came round to our house with some special wax crayons for Hannah (big mistake: remember Snow White's stepmother's purple robe) and some rainbow metallic pens for me. The next Saturday, surprise surprise, we just happened to bump into Miss Morgan in the children's library. We all chatted for a bit and then we took Hannah to the swings and

then we all had lunch in McDonald's. Before we knew what was happening we were seeing Miss Morgan every single Saturday and sometimes Sundays too.

I didn't mind a bit at first. I know this makes me the most seriously stupid, dumb dolthead but there you are. Even poor William would have twigged what was going on – but I thought Miss Morgan was *my* friend. And Hannah's too, of course. I didn't *dream* that she was there because of our dad.

Miss Morgan is as pretty as a princess. Our dad  doesn't look a bit like a handsome prince. Well, not the ones in my fairy-tale book. They don't wear baggy T-shirts and tracksuit bottoms and fluffy socks with holes in the toes. Though Dad got all dressed up in a suit on Friday night.

'I'm going out, girls. I've asked Auntie Evie up the road to babysit.'

'We don't need Auntie Evie. She fusses too much,' I said, pulling a face. '*I'll* babysit for Hannah, Dad.'

'I know you're just like a little mother to Hannah, love, but I'd feel happier if Auntie Evie was here to keep an eye on things,' said Dad, tying the knot in the funny *Simpsons* tie Hannah and I gave him last birthday. He only wears his tie if he's going somewhere really special.

'Are you going out somewhere posh with your mates from work, Dad?' I asked.

'No, love,' said Dad, sprucing his hair in the mirror. 'Why does it always stick straight up?'

'Maybe you need some hair gel, Dad.'

He peered in the mirror, his head at an odd angle. 'You don't think I'm going thin on top, do you, Holly?'

'Yeah, like you're almost totally bald,' I said, teasing him. 'Leave it out, Dad, you've got lovely thick hair.'

'You're a great little kid, Holly,' said Dad, giving me a hug.

'So where *are* you going, Dad?'

Dad looked in the mirror rather than at me. 'I'm taking Jenny out for a meal.'

'Jenny?'

Dad went red.

'You know. Miss Morgan.'

I stared at him. Hannah bounced up.

'A meal? Can we come too? Can we go to McDonald's?' Hannah begged.

'No, no, you wouldn't want to come, Hannah. We're going to this Italian place.'

'I like Italian food. I like spaghetti,' Hannah insisted.

'Well, maybe you and Holly can come with us another time. But this is a meal just for grown-ups,' said Dad.

'It's a *date*,' I said. I spat the word out as if it was deadly poison. 'You and Miss Morgan. You're going *out* with her!'

'You don't mind, do you?' said Dad. 'You *like* Jenny – Miss Morgan.'

'We *love* her,' said Hannah. 'Oh, Dad, is she your girlfriend now?'

'Well . . . sort of,' said Dad, positively beetroot.

'Oh great, great, great!' Hannah shouted. 'Here Dad, why don't you marry Miss Morgan and then she can be our mum!'

'Not so fast, Teeny Tiny Girlfriend,' said Dad, and he picked Hannah up and swung her round and round. Her feet flew out and her left Pokémon slipper clunked me straight on the head.

I made a lot of fuss though my head didn't really hurt a bit. It was inside me that was hurting. My dad – and Miss Morgan!

'What's up, Big Grown-up Girlfriend?' said Dad. 'Is your head really sore? Shall I kiss it better?'

'I'm not a baby. Don't be so daft,' I snapped. 'Save your kissing for Miss Morgan.'

Dad looked like I'd thrown a bucket of cold water all over him. He blinked at me.

'I thought you'd be dead chuffed like Hannah,' he said. 'You *like* Jenny, Holly. I don't get it.'

I didn't really get it either. I just knew it was all spoilt now. And *I* carried on spoiling it. We still went out every Saturday, but I mucked it up. I sighed and fussed and moaned in the children's library. Whenever Miss Morgan picked out some book she thought I might enjoy I'd glance at it and give a big yawn and go, 'Boring!' So she found picture books for Hannah instead. Dad and Miss Morgan sat squashed together on one of those silly saggy cushion chairs, with Hannah tucked under their chins looking at the pictures in the book. They looked like a real family already.

The girl behind the counter in McDonald's thought they were a family too. Hannah jumped up and said she wanted a giant portion of French fries and *five* ice creams and the girl laughed and looked at Miss Morgan and said, 'Perhaps we'd better ask Mum first.'

'She's not our mum,' I said fiercely. When we sat down with our food I thumped my plastic tray so hard my milk shake tipped and trickled all over me, and quite a bit of Miss Morgan too.

'For goodness' sake, Holly, what's the matter with you?' said Dad, mopping at Miss Morgan with his paper napkin. He just let me drip. 'You're behaving like a total idiot.'

'You're the total idiot,' I muttered. Not softly enough.

'I've just about had enough of you, showing me up and behaving so badly,' Dad hissed.

'Here, Holly, let's go to the Ladies' and get some paper towels,' said Miss Morgan in a friendly but very firm teacher's voice, so I couldn't quite manage to say no. When we were in the Ladies' she didn't mess around with the milk-shake stains. She put her hands on my shoulders and looked me straight in the eyes.

'It's OK, Holly. I understand the way you feel.'

'No, you don't,' I said sulkily.

 I didn't see how she could understand when *I* didn't have a clue why I felt so bad and was acting bad into the bargain.

'I like your dad – and he seems to like me,' said Miss Morgan.

'Yuck!' I said.

'Yes, OK, it seems very yucky to you. It probably would to me too if I was in the same situation.'

The *really* yucky thing was she was being so nicey-nicey-nice to me, *sooooo* soft and sweet. It made me feel fiercer than ever.

'I promise you, I'm not trying to take the place of your mum. I know just how much she means to you. She'll always stay your mum – and Hannah's – for ever and ever, even though you don't see her any more.'

'We do *so* see her!' I shouted. 'We see her lots and lots and lots, so you can just shut up and stay away from me and my family.'

I rushed into a cubicle and locked the door and wouldn't come out for ages. In fact *Dad* had to come into the Ladies' to get me out and it was dead embarrassing and everyone was staring.

I managed to hold things in until I was in bed that night and then I cried and cried and cried. I tried to cry quietly but I woke Hannah.

'Are you crying because you've been so bad?' she whispered. She had been awestruck by my behaviour.

'I'm *not* crying. I've just got a cold,' I snuffled, blowing my nose.

I really did get a cold the next day and I made such a fuss that Dad let me stay off school. Auntie Evie up the road came to keep an eye on me. When she dozed off watching *Neighbours* after lunch I crept into the hall and made a phone call – to my mum.

Mum didn't know who I was at first.

Well, she *did*. She just didn't recognize my voice and said, 'Who?' suspiciously as if it was someone playing a joke on her.

'It's *me*, Mum.' I paused. I wondered if I was going to have to add, '*You* know. Holly. Your *daughter*.'

'What do you want, Holly? Is something wrong?'

'No. Yes. It's Dad.'

'Well, what about him? He's not ill, is he? Because I can't really have you girls to stay at the moment as

I'm not too great myself and I'm having all sorts of dramas with Mike and . . .'

She went on and on and on. Then she remembered.

'Anyway. What about your dad?'

'He's got a *girlfriend*!'

'Has he?' She sounded so casual, as if I'd just announced he'd got a new tie.

'She's a teacher at our school.'

'Oh well. That figures. It's the only way your dad would ever meet anyone.'

I hated the way Mum always sounded so sniffy about Dad, like he was the most boring man on earth.

'Don't you mind, Mum?'

'Well, what's it got to do with me?'

'It's serious. She might end up our stepmother.'

'Oh! Isn't she very nice to you then?'

'She's . . .' I couldn't quite tell an outright lie. 'She's OK.'

'Then what are you worried about, eh?'

'Well, she *could* turn out horrid. Most stepmothers are. Like in "Snow White".'

'Ah. "Snow White". I had that fairy-tale book when I was a little girl.'

'I *know*. You gave it to me.'

I can't stand it when Mum forgets things. Sometimes it feels as if she's forgotten all about me. I wanted to tell her how much I loved her and missed her but the words wouldn't sort themselves out and while I was still wondering how to say it Mum said, 'Well, I've got to go now, Holly. See you. Bye.'

So I put the phone down. I stopped feeling I loved her and hated her for a bit. She said 'see you' but she doesn't want to. She doesn't even like talking to me on the phone much now.

Dad says it's because she feels bad about leaving us. I think maybe *she's* bad.

I take after her now.

I went back to school the next day because it was dead depressing staying at home. My nose was sniffier than ever and so was I. Samantha was showing off her new hair slides, which were like little butterflies, but I simply yawned and said they looked stupid. Samantha said I was just jealous because she had long fair curls  and I didn't. I said I didn't care one bit about having long fair curls. (*Big* lie.) Greg said he didn't think long fair curls were all that great and he much

26

preferred *my* hair! Old Greg is going as daft as poor William if you ask me.

Mr Speed told me to hand the marked homework out and asked me to read aloud to the others and sent me with a message to the Head. I bashed the homework books bang on the desks, I read aloud in a bored, flat, can't-be-bothered voice, and I dawdled down the corridor so slowly after giving my message I missed half the lesson.

'I wonder why you're in such a bad mood today, Holly?' said Mr Speed.

I shrugged and pouted. Mr Speed imitated me. He looked so funny I very nearly gave in and giggled.

'Maybe you need a bit of peace and quiet? I know! How about a little computer practice?'

I knew this was a Crafty Ploy. Mr Speed wanted me to access his Worry Website. And I couldn't resist. I typed it in. Remember?

I think I'm going to get a stepmother.

I wish she was wicked.

Comments:

You're nuts!

27

What is she on about?

How do you know the person with the worry is a girl?

Because it's such a silly girly thing.

You're being dead sexist.

Look, what about his/her PROBLEM?

What problem? Heaps of kids get stepmothers. I've got one and she's OK.

I've got a mum and a dad and a stepmum and a stepdad and it's great at Christmas and birthdays because you get two lots of presents.

Why do you want a WICKED stepmother???

I've GOT a wicked stepmother. You can have mine!

I didn't think these comments particularly kind. Or constructive. There were other even more useless suggestions that I deleted. I sat staring at the screen, wishing I could delete myself. Mr Speed saw me and whizzed right over before I could quit the website.

'Aha! So you're having a peep at the Worry Website, Holly. Hmm. Interesting worry! Have you typed in your comment for this poor soul who wants a wicked stepmother?'

He was trying to kid me that the website is ultra-anonymous. But I'm not daft. I gave him a long hard look.

'I'm the poor soul, Mr Speed. You know it's me.'

'Yes, that's very true, Holly. You've caught me out.'

'*You* haven't put a comment.'

'That's also true. OK.' He leaned over me and typed.

I don't know WHY you want a wicked stepmother. Perhaps you can elaborate?

He waited. I fidgeted.

'Elaborate means tell me more,' said Mr Speed.

'I know. I don't know *how* though. It's all muddly. It's my dad – and Miss Morgan.'

Mr Speed's eyes opened wide.

'*Our* Miss Morgan?'

'This is highly confidential, Mr Speed,' I said hurriedly.

'Mum's the word,' said Mr Speed, finger on his lips.

So I told him. His eyes got wider and wider, like the dog in the fairy tale with eyes as big as dinner plates.

'Your dad's a very lucky man,' he said eventually. 'And I should imagine young Hannah's thrilled. So . . . how do you feel, Holly?'

'I feel bad,' I said. 'And I keep acting bad and then I feel even worse. And Miss Morgan is always so nicey-nicey-nice about it. I want *her* to be bad. If she was really wicked like Snow White's stepmother

29

then I could hate her and be horrid to her and it would be perfectly OK.'

'I can't *quite* imagine Miss Morgan trying to force you to eat poisoned apples,' said Mr Speed. 'Let alone hiring an axeman to chop you into little bits in the middle of the forest.'

'I think I've got a worry that can't be solved,' I said gloomily.

'Well . . . we could just fiddle with the meaning of wicked. I've always thought Miss Morgan an ultra-lovely, delightful young woman – this is also highly confidential, Holly. I especially admire her amazing purple boots. We could well say she looks seriously wicked. Right?'

I groaned.

'Sorry!' Mr Speed shook his head at me apologetically. 'I'll work on it. But there aren't always easy answers to worries. You know that. Tell you something though. You're *not* bad. You're still my little star. You'll get your twinkle back soon, you'll see.'

I kept out of Miss Morgan's way that week. I delivered Hannah off at the door of the Reception class but didn't go in myself. Dad went out with Miss Morgan on Friday night but he came home early when I was still sitting up in bed reading my fairy-tale book. He popped his head round the door to tell me to put the light off and go to sleep. He seemed all sad and scowly. Maybe he'd had a row with Miss Morgan!

However, she came round to our house on Saturday looking extra-specially lovely in a long purple dress with little mirrors all round the hem.

'Let me see if I can see my face,' said Hannah, kneeling down and peering into each mirror. 'Mirror, mirror, on the wall, who is the fairest of them all?'

'Mirror, mirror on her skirt, who is acting like a stupid little squirt?' I said, yanking Hannah upright.

'Ouch! You're so grumpy now, Holly. I don't want you to come round the town with us because you spoil everything,' said Hannah.

'Good, I don't *want* to come,' I said, but I felt bad, bad, bad. My eyes went all watery because even Hannah didn't want me any more.

'I think we won't *all* go round the town today,'

said Miss Morgan. Her eyes were as glittery as the little mirrors on her skirt. 'Maybe Holly and I might just go shopping together?'

'What about *me*?' said Hannah indignantly.

'I'll take you to the library and the swings, Hannah, and then we'll have an ice cream or two – or three or four or five – in McDonald's, OK?' said Dad.

Hannah had her mouth open to protest bitterly but she got sidetracked by the ice-cream bribe. Maybe my mouth was open too. I didn't get what was going on.

'I don't want to go shopping,' I said.

'Yes, you do – if you've got money in your pocket,' said Dad, and he handed me a ten-pound note.

I couldn't believe it. Ten pounds, all for me! So I sloped off with Miss Morgan. I decided I wasn't going to speak to her though. Not one word, all the way into town. But the weird thing was, she didn't say one word to me either! She just strode along in her purple pointy boots and whenever I glanced at her she *glared* at me. I'd never seen her glare before, not even when Hannah's Reception class got really, really rowdy and started throwing powder paint about. (It might have been Hannah who started it because she ended up rainbow-coloured right down to her knickers.)

It's sort of scary when a smiley person goes all glarey. The silence was starting to get on my nerves so much that I blurted out, 'I want to go to Claire's Accessories to get some of those little butterfly slides. And maybe one of those little lucky-bead bracelets.'

Miss Morgan sniffed. 'You're lucky all right, Holly. Your dad spoils you so. And you've certainly been acting like a spoilt brat recently. I'm getting sick of it.'

I stared at her. It was as if she'd suddenly started spitting toads.

'You're not supposed to talk to me like that. You're a *teacher*!'

'And I'm also your dad's girlfriend and if you'd only give us a chance I think we'd be really happy together. But you just want to muck everything up, don't you? Can't you see how unhappy you're making your dad?'

'He's only unhappy because of *you*. *You've* mucked everything up. It was really great before, when it was just Hannah and Dad and me.'

'*You* felt great,' said Miss Morgan, and she stamped her boot so that her skirt swung and all the little mirrors glittered. 'Don't you realize how *lonely* your dad felt?'

'He wasn't a bit lonely! And anyway, maybe – maybe my mum might come back and then he'd have *her*, wouldn't he?'

'You know perfectly well your mum isn't ever going to come back. And even if she did your dad wouldn't want her. She walked out on all of you, even little Hannah. I don't see how she could ever have done that. Why do you act like she's so wonderful when she could do a wicked thing like leave her own children?'

'*You're* wicked and I hate you! I wish you'd stomp off in your silly boots and never ever come back!' Tears spilled down my cheeks. 'Why did you have to turn out so horrible?'

'Oh, Holly!' said Miss Morgan. Tears streamed down her cheeks too. 'I'm sorry. I *am* wicked. I don't want to be horrible. I can't do this any more. It's awful. I like you too much.'

'No you don't! No-one does. No-one wants me!'

'I want you very, very much,' she said.

She put her arms round me and we hugged right there in the street. I cried and she cried. We kept on hugging. I sniffled so much I dripped on her purple dress but she didn't mind a bit. She found her hankie and I blew my nose and she blew her nose too and then we went off to this posh coffee shop and had wonderful grown-up frothy coffee and an apple Danish pastry each. I had difficulty eating mine at first because I had hiccups from all that crying. Miss Morgan saw me hesitating.

'They're not poisoned apples, I promise,' she said.

I peered at her suspiciously, spooning up the froth from my coffee.

'What's Mr Speed been saying to you?'

'Mr Speed?' said Miss Morgan, dead nonchalant. She shook her head, tossing her lovely long hair over her shoulder. 'Oh, nothing in particular.'

You know what teachers are like. They always back each other up.

I think Mr Speed *might* have told her my Worry, even though it's supposed to be confidential. He was just trying to act like a fairy godmother and grant my

wish. I had a sudden vision of Mr Speed in a fairy frock clutching a wand and I laughed so much I blew the rest of my froth off my coffee.

'What?' said Miss Morgan, giggling a bit too.

'Oh, nothing in particular,' I said. I thought for a bit. 'Miss Morgan – I'm sorry I said all that stuff. I don't really hate you.'

'I'm sorry too, Holly. I didn't mean all that stuff I said either. I was just feeling fed up and worried because your dad said on Friday that we might have to stop seeing each other if it was making you so unhappy. He always puts you and Hannah first.'

'Well . . . you come second,' I said, patting her hand. 'And I'll tell Dad I don't really want you two to break up.'

'Yes, you might end up with a *really* wicked stepmother,' said Miss Morgan, and she pulled this dreadful frowny ferocious face.

I laughed and she laughed – and we both knew we'd kind of made friends. They never seem to do that in fairy stories, do they? Then we

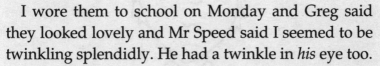 went shopping and I bought Miss Morgan a little comb for her long thick hair and I got Dad some gel for his short thinning hair. I found some butterfly slides but I bought them for Hannah. I chose special little gold star slides for me. Miss Morgan said they really, really suited me.

I wore them to school on Monday and Greg said they looked lovely and Mr Speed said I seemed to be twinkling splendidly. He had a twinkle in *his* eye too.

Miss Morgan said she's going to make Hannah and me special dresses. Hannah's is going to have little mirrors and mine is going to have stars embroidered all over.

I suppose they could just be bridesmaid's dresses . . .

GREG'S WORRY

Type in your worry:

Oh dear. I hope no-one's looking. This is so embarrassing. OK. Here goes.

I like this girl. I like her very much. I want to be her friend. I want to be her BOYfriend. I've gone all red and shuddery and yucky just typing it! I hate all this lovey-dovey stuff. It really sucks. I don't WANT to feel like this. I generally HATE girls.

I certainly hate my sister Sarah-Jane. She is only a year younger than me but she's little and dinky-looking and she talks in a special lispy baby voice so that everyone treats her like she's five years old.

It's so irritating having a *little* sister. She's allowed to kick me or elbow me in the ribs or creep up behind me and pinch my neck but if I clump her one I'm in serious trouble. I'm *generally* in serious trouble at home about Sarah-Jane.

She's so sneaky too. She puts on this little simper and says, 'Mum, I don't want to be mean and tell on Greg, but—' and then she *does* tell. She exaggerates like crazy. And then Mum bellows, 'Gregory!' and I know I'm for it. I *hate* being called Gregory. It's a saint's name. You certainly need the patience of a saint with Sarah-Jane as your sister.

I don't like my girl cousins much either, Yvonne and Julia and Katrina. They come round our house on a Sunday and they all squeeze into Sarah-Jane's bedroom and try on each other's clothes and do each other's hair. They do this for *hours*. Then I have to sit with them for Sunday lunch and they go whisper, whisper, whisper, giggle, giggle, giggle. It is *torture*. I feel so tense about it that I can't eat comfortably and that makes me do certain rude

windy things and then they all squeal and Mum goes, *'Gregory!'* as if I'm doing it on purpose. Which just occasionally I am.

I didn't reckon any of the girls in my class at school either. Well, Claire's OK because she's good at football and I suppose I've always thought Samantha's ever so pretty – but she reminds me too much of Sarah-Jane. I never really noticed any of the other girls.

But then I got to sit behind Holly when we all went into Mr Speed's class. I stuck my feet on the back of her chair and kicked a bit, because that's what you *do* when a girl sits in front of you. Most of them whine and fidget and moan that you're getting mud on their skirt. But Holly whipped round quick as a wink, her fingers went fiddly-flick – and there were my shoelaces tied together! Then she gave me this great grin. I couldn't help grinning back even though she'd tied such a tight knot I couldn't pick it open and had to saw through my shoelaces with my penknife.

40

I don't know how to put it into words. It was just her big grin. It really got to me.

So I tried to figure out ways of making her grin again. The next day I came to school wearing my muddy walks-in-the-country welly boots. We don't often *go* for muddy walks in the country so they'd got a bit small without my realizing. I had to scrunch up my toes, which was dead uncomfortable. I also had to put up with everyone asking me why I was wearing my wellies when it wasn't raining. Not so much as a cloud in the sky.

Mr Speed did this whole pantomime thing of putting up an imaginary umbrella. Everyone laughed. Holly laughed too. I waited until everyone stopped sniggering at my boring foot-blistering boots. Mr Speed started telling some soppy fairy story in the Literacy Hour and Holly was listening hard, her hair tucked behind her neat little ears. *Then* I put my boots on the back of her chair.

She turned round.

I waited. I thought she'd see she couldn't tie any laces this time and give that glorious grin again. But she sighed, stiffened her hand, and gave the tip of each boot a swift karate chop.

 It was such AGONY on my poor rubbed tootsies that I screamed. 'Oh my goodness, Greg!' Mr Speed exploded, clutching his chest. 'You'll give me a heart attack. I hope you have a totally convincing excuse for that banshee wail. Are you being fiendishly attacked by invisible aliens?'

'No, Mr Speed,' I mumbled, trying to ease my throbbing feet.

'Then why the scream? Is it National Torment Mr Speed Day today? No, that's *every* day as far as you lot are concerned. I warn you, children, I am in a very savage mood today. I am becoming more savage every second, moodier every minute. Well, Greg, I'm waiting for your explanation. I've given you long enough to concoct one. Were you perhaps provoked in some way?'

'No, Mr Speed,' I said firmly. 'I was just messing about.'

Holly turned round and gave me a quick smile, an abbreviated text-message version of her gorgeous grin.

I'd have listened to Mr Speed lecturing me all day long just for that one weeny glance.

But it didn't get me anywhere.

I tried coming to school in my bedroom slippers the next day. My poor sore feet needed a little bit of cosseting. Unfortunately *this* time it decided to rain. In fact it positively poured buckets and my slippers got sodden.

I had to lie down on my back at the side of the classroom and rest both soaking slippers on the radiators until they steamed. Mr Speed came in late and pretended to trip right over me.

'I've always assumed that standard classroom posture is bottom on chair. Is there any reason why you prefer this lying-on-back, legs-in-air position, Greg?' Mr Speed said wearily.

I told him I was simply trying to dry out my slippers.

'Ah, I wondered what that extraordinary smell was,' said Mr Speed. 'Feet *off* the radiator, please! You'll give yourself chilblains as well as stinking the place out. I'm beginning to find your inappropriate footwear fetish rather irritating, lad. I suggest you turn up in standard sensible shoes tomorrow or you *might* just find yourself left behind in the classroom when we go off on the school trip.'

The school trip! It wasn't anything to get excited about in itself. We were just going to a musty old museum. But we travelled there by coach! I had to find some way of sitting next to Holly on the journey.

She's got lots and lots and lots of friends in our class, but she hasn't got one *particular* friend. I was in with a chance. But she could pick anyone. There are thirty children in our class so she could have her choice of twenty-nine of us.

I wondered *how* I could get her to pick me.

I sauntered past the computer dead casually and then looked at my worry on the website to see if anyone had given me any good tips about getting a girlfriend.

Ha ha ha. I am not laughing. I am being extremely sarcastic. There weren't any tips at all, just a whole load of rubbish.

Comments:

I hate girls too.

So do I. They've got such silly squeaky voices that they make your head ache when they go on at you. And they don't understand important stuff like football.

Oh yes they do! I bet I know who you are and you're lousy at football. I don't want to boast but I'm in the football team even though I'm a girl and I scored three goals last match so you shut up.

See! They go on at you! You've proved my point.

I bet none of the girls in our class would go out with any of the boys because the boys are all so childish and stupid. I hate BOYS.

Some of the boys are OK. I would like one boy in particular to be my boyfriend. Guess who I am!

My heart leapt when I read that one, but this person had added her name at the end. Not her full name because we're not allowed to. So she put S——————a.

Well, even weird William would have no trouble at all working that one out.

'Aha!' said Mr Speed, peering over my shoulder.

I felt my cheeks burning, as if someone had switched on an electric fire in my face. My glasses steamed up so I could hardly see.

'This is a daft worry,' I said quickly. 'I don't

know what sort of idiot would write that.'

'*My* sort of idiot,' said Mr Speed. He scrolled through the answers. 'Oh dear! They're not very sympathetic, are they? I'd hoped they might have some kind of constructive advice for this poor lovelorn chap. *I* need advice.'

'Are you in love, Mr Speed?' I asked, astonished. I mean, Mr Speed is a *teacher*. And he's old too. Well, I think he is. It's difficult to tell with grown-ups. It's easy enough to tell whether a kid is five or ten or fifteen – but how do I know whether Mr Speed is twenty-five or thirty or thirty-five or even *older*.

'Don't stare at me like that, lad. I'm not ready for my pension yet,' said Mr Speed sharply.

'How do you read people's minds, Mr Speed?' I said.

'Oh, it's my laser-light bionic glasses,' said Mr Speed, wrinkling his nose so that his glasses wiggled about.

I laughed and wiggled my own glasses back.

'Mr Speed, do you think girls mind if boys wear glasses?' I said.

'I don't think they mind a bit,' said Mr Speed. He struck a silly pose. 'I've never found it a deterrent.'

'But you're having problems now, Mr Speed?

'Indeed I am, Greg. In the presence of a certain lady I go all red and shuddery and yucky, to quote these expressive words on the website.'

'And do you think this lady will be your girlfriend, Mr Speed?'

'Alas and alack, her heart belongs to another,' said Mr Speed. 'So *my* heart is broken!' He thumped himself on the chest and groaned. He didn't *mean* it. He's always carrying on like that. He's a bit nuts if you ask me.

'*However*,' Mr Speed said, with emphasis, 'the lovelorn boy with the current worry on the website should not be downhearted. It looks like his lovely little lady friend is making it particularly plain that she cares for him.'

I blinked. I backtracked through his speech. He talks in such a funny way that this is necessary sometimes.

'You mean you think I – he – is in with a chance?' I said excitedly.

'Definitely. She couldn't be making it plainer. What more do you want, lad? Does she have to stand on a desktop and proclaim her love to the entire class?'

I thought about it.

'I'd quite like that,' I said.

'Mmm, so would I!' said Mr Speed, laughing. 'But I don't think she'll be quite as bold as all that.'

'So you think she'd maybe sit next to this boy on the school trip?'

'You bet. He should just *ask* her,' said Mr Speed.

So I did.

I couldn't quite get up the courage until we were all set to go and Mr Speed was taking the register. Then I very gently nudged Holly with my shoe.

She turned round, sighed elaborately, and started undoing one of my new laces.

'Don't Holly, please! My mum will go spare. I had to nick *these* laces out of our Sarah-Jane's Irish dancing shoes.'

'Well, quit kicking me then,' Holly hissed.

'I'm not kicking, I'm attracting your attention.'

'Oh yeah?' said Holly. She looked straight into my eyes. 'Why?'

I went red and shuddery and yuckety-yucky *but* I looked straight back at her and said it. 'Will you sit next to me on the coach?'

'OK,' said Holly, like it was no big deal at all. Then she grinned.

I felt I was shooting straight through the classroom ceiling up into the bright blue sky.

Then Mr Speed told us to line up for the coach. Everyone surged forward, out of the classroom, along the corridor, out of the door, across the playground, out of the gate to where the school coach was waiting. But I hung back with Holly, grinning and grinning at her. And she grinned back.

Mr Speed was herding everyone onto the coach. He called to us to hurry up. Then he caught hold of me.

'Here's your chance, boy,' he said, and he propelled me forwards, up the big steps and onto the front seat . . . next to *Samantha*!

'Hi, Greg,' she said, smiling at me. 'I've saved this seat for you.'

I stared at her in horror.

'But I'm sitting next to—'

'Samantha!' commanded Mr Speed. He seized me by the shoulders and sat me down on the front seat beside her. 'Don't be bashful, lad,' he whispered in my ear. 'Take this golden opportunity.'

'But Mr Speed, you've got it all *wrong*,' I wailed. 'I don't *like* Samantha.'

Mr Speed was hurrying up and down the coach aisle checking on purses and packed lunches and sick bags and didn't even hear me.

But Samantha did.

She looked amazed. Then appalled. Her blue eyes went all watery. I felt horrible.

'I didn't mean I don't *like* you, Samantha. Of course I do. You're *ever* so nice, but it's just there's this other girl I like better.'

I seemed to be making it worse.

'Well, I don't like *you*,' she said. 'Get off this seat! I wouldn't sit next to you if you went down on your knees and *begged*.'

'Fat chance,' I said. I jumped up – but Mr Speed rushed past and gave me a shove down again.

'Up and down, up and down, like a jack-in-the-box,' he said. 'Sit *still*, Greg.'

'But I don't want to sit next to Samantha, Mr Speed!'

'He's certainly *not* sitting next to me!'

Mr Speed stopped, hands on hips. He breathed in deeply. This is generally a warning signal.

'Well well well! I was under

the impression *I* was the teacher and *you* were the pupils, but I've obviously got that entirely wrong, because here you are giving *me* the orders.' He paused ominously. 'Are you the teacher here, Gregory?'

'No, Mr Speed.'

'What about you, Samantha?'

'No, Mr Speed.'

'Then, my goodness, *I* must be the teacher. And I say sit down in your seats and do not utter another word or I will sit on you myself.'

I didn't utter a word to Samantha and she didn't utter a word to me for the entire journey. We weren't on speaking terms.

I tried kneeling on my seat to see Holly. I tried to attract Holly's attention. I failed. I attracted Mr Speed's attention instead. This was a *big* mistake.

He made me stick with him all the way round the museum, while all the others were allowed to ramble around in little groups having fun. I called after Holly but she stared straight past me as if she couldn't even see me.

'You're an exceptionally aggravating boy, Gregory,' said Mr Speed. 'Why do you have to be so fickle with your affections? First you declare undying love for Samantha and yet when I give you the opportunity to sit next to her you behave totally offensively and transfer your affections to Holly.'

'I *never*,' I mumbled despairingly.

'That sounds ungrammatical but heartfelt,' said Mr Speed, peering at me. 'Explain yourself, lad.'

'It was Holly all the time, Mr Speed. You got it all wrong.'

'I got it all wrong, did I?' said Mr Speed.

I wondered if I was in for another lecture, but he was shaking his head. 'Sorry, lad. I obviously jumped to the wrong conclusions. The old bionic glasses went all smeary on me. I'd better not try to play Cupid again.'

But he *did*!

After we'd trailed all round the museum we went into a special room where a lady got out this big trunk of Victorian clothes and we all had to dress up and look daft. Mr Speed put on a top hat and a funny false moustache and then unearthed a pair of button boots from the bottom of the trunk.

'I know a lad who's into fancy footwear,'

he said. 'Here, Greg, put them on.'

They were nearly the right size but I couldn't get them buttoned up at all. They were far too fiddly.

'You need a buttonhook,' said the museum lady, producing this weird metal pointy thing with a bone handle.

'Aha! Let's pop this mob cap and pinny on you, Holly. You can be young Master Gregory's nursery maid,' said Mr Speed. 'Button the lad into his boots then, girl.'

'Certainly, Mr Speed,' said Holly. She seized the buttonhook as if it was a surgical instrument.

I didn't like the look of her grin at all now!

'Keep still, now,' she said,  and she went *prod*, *prod*, *prod*. And *I* went 'Ow! Ow! Ow!'

'Don't be a silly baby, Master Gregory,' said Holly.

'OW! Cut it out, Holly! You're prodding right into my *leg*,' I protested.

'Good,' said Holly, under her breath. 'Why did you go and sit next to that stupid Samantha?'

'I didn't want to! It was all Mr Speed's fault. He made me. You know what he's like.'

'I know what *you're* like,' said Holly.

I swallowed. I took a very deep breath. I went all red and shuddery and yuckety-yuckety-yucky.

'But do you know *who* I like?' I said.

Holly looked at me, twiddling the buttonhook.

Then she grinned. I grinned back.

Guess who I got to sit next to on the coach going home!

And guess who is now my girlfriend!

Holly!

CLAIRE'S WORRY

Type in your worry:

I have this nightmare. It's really, really scary. I don't know what to do. I dream it every single night. Does anyone else have nightmares or am I the only one?

I've had bad dreams before. I've dreamt I've been walking to school and suddenly I'm just wearing my knickers and everyone starts staring and pointing and giggling. I always feel silly going to school the next day, as if it had really happened!

 I've also had a falling dream. I'm at the top of this very long escalator and I suddenly trip and I go tumbling down and down and down . . . until I wake up with a start.

Then there's that dream when I'm having a huge row with my sister Judy in our bedroom. She's bigger and bossier than me but I bash her with my pillow and she falls flat on her bed. She doesn't move. I think she's just pretending she's hurt to scare me but my pillow feels strangely heavy and when I look inside I find it's full of rocks.

These are all pretty horrible dreams but they're not *too* bad. I don't think about them all the time. I can make sure they don't really happen. I can check I'm wearing my school uniform, avoid all escalators, and stop bashing Judy with my pillow. Well, I *do* still have pillow fights with her but they're mostly in fun. I have a quick pummel of the pillow first to make sure it's totally rock-free.

But now I'm having this new nightmare. I dream it every night. It's awful.

I've tried getting into Judy's bed. She moaned and fussed and said I was squashing her. It didn't work anyway. I still had the nightmare. I woke up screaming. Judy woke up too.

'What are you playing at, Claire? You woke me up! Hey, are you crying?'

'No,' I sobbed.

'Yes, you are,' said Judy. She suddenly put her arms round me. 'Shall I get Mum?'

'*No!*'

This is the trouble. I can't tell Mum or Dad. They will say it's all my own fault. And I suppose it is.

You see I secretly watched this ultra-scary video. Mum and Dad are quite strict about what films we're allowed to see. Especially me. I don't know what's the matter with me. I've always been so stupid. When I was a really little kid I sometimes got scared watching *cartoons*! There's a bit where horses gallop wildly in *Beauty and the Beast* that made me have bad dreams. I used to wake up crying that the horses were after me. My big brother Michael used to neigh and make galloping noises just to get me going.

Mum got fed up getting up to go to me in the night so ever since she's been very picky over what I'm allowed to watch. I kept telling her and telling her that I wasn't a silly baby any more. I was furious when she let Michael and Judy watch *Titanic* but she wouldn't let *me*.

'Of course you can't watch it, Claire. You'd dream you were drowning and then you'd wet the bed,' Michael chortled.

I hated being left out. I knew silly old movies couldn't scare me any more. Or so I thought.

But then I watched *The Monster*. I wonder if you've seen it? It's been a *big* talking point at our school. Heaps of kids go on about how great it is and say it's the scariest film ever, ever, ever. Some kids say it didn't scare *them* one bit. I think they're fibbing. I bet they haven't seen so much as the trailer.

I got to see it on Saturday. Mum and Judy had gone up to London because she had a music exam and then they were going shoe shopping afterwards.

I was supposed to go too but I made a fuss. I *hate* listening while Judy plays her violin. She sounds like chalk squeaking on a blackboard. I have to put my fingers in my ears and then Judy says I'm putting her off deliberately. And shoe shopping is *soooo* boring, unless you're looking for something cool like football boots or trainers.

So I stayed at home with Dad and Michael. Michael had his friend, Luke, round. They usually go into Michael's room and try to access rude things on the Internet, *I* know. But Dad was outside washing and polishing the car which takes him for ever, so Luke casually produced the video of *The Monster* from his backpack.

'Fancy watching a bit, Mike?'

'Wow!' said Michael, eyes goggling. 'You bet!'

'I'm watching too,' I said.

'There's no way *you're* watching, baby,' said Michael. He tried to push me out the living room while Luke slotted the video into the machine.

'There's *every* way I'm watching it – or I'll tell Dad,' I said.

I don't *like* being a telltale but when you have bossy big brothers and sisters you have to use any means at your disposal to get your own way.

So I won. I watched *The Monster*. Well, nearly half of it. Then we heard Dad coming back inside the house so we switched over to a sports programme, sharpish.

You have no idea how appalling *The Monster* is.

Far, far, far, *far* worse than you can ever imagine. I kept on telling myself it was just a silly old film. It wasn't a *real* monster. But it looked so real when it rose up out of the river, sickly green, oozing slime, and semi-transparent so you could see all its horrible heart and liver and lungs and long long coils of intestines, some of them hanging *out* and spurting terrible sludgy streams of poo.

Luke whooped with laughter, but it was very high-pitched. Michael started biting his nails. The

Monster started oozing up out of sinks and baths and even *toilets*. It devoured everything – dogs, cats, babies in buggies, screaming schoolchildren, frantic mothers, fighting fathers. The Monster even swallowed this huge fat man and you *saw* him being digested inside it, getting covered in bile, bits disintegrating before your very eyes.

Luke stopped laughing. Michael nearly bit his fingers right off. I stared at the screen helplessly, unable to move. The Monster seemed to ooze right out of the television set into my head. It was there, pulsing inside my brain, ready to ooze its way into my dreams.

They are the worst nightmares ever. I don't know what I'm going to do. I start feeling vaguely sick at teatime. I go out in the garden and play afterwards but all the time I'm kicking a football about or running up and down with my skipping rope I'm thinking about the Monster. When I'm watching television It's there too, slithering into Central Perk and nibbling Phoebe and Rachel and Monica like sweets.

Then Mum starts nagging that it's time for bed and the Monster is lurking on the stairs, in the bathroom, under my bed. Dad comes to read to Judy and me but the Monster paces the corridors of Hogwarts too, munching Harry Potter into mincemeat.

After Dad tucks us up and puts the light out I whisper to Judy, desperate to keep her awake. I talk about all the boy bands she's currently nuts on and the new boots she wants in Bertie's and the boy on the bike who waves to her every morning and whether this means he really fancies her. This is all terminally boring, boring, boring but it means Judy will keep chatting to me. But no matter how I try to keep the conversation going eventually she starts mumbling nonsense and then she sighs and gives a little snore. She is asleep, dreaming about boys and bands and bikes and boots.

I struggle to stay awake because I know what *I'm* going to dream about. I hear Michael go to bed. Sometimes I even hear Mum and Dad go to bed. I play the silliest games to stop myself sleeping. I go through all my favourites.

Hero: David Beckham.
Friend: Holly, and Lisa's OK too.
Hobby: football.
Teacher: Mr Speed.
Colour: anything but slime green.

But no matter which rainbow hue I choose this sickening slime green oozes over it and I'm dreaming the Monster is coming to get me. I dream it every single night.

I waited to see if anyone typed in anything helpful on the Worry Website. There were *heaps* of comments. Everyone said they had nightmares too. I counted. There were thirty. That meant every single person in the class. No, wait a minute. *I* didn't comment on my own worry.

Mr Speed saw me scrolling down the screen, re-counting.

'I'm glad to see you practising your maths as well as your IT skills, Claire.'

'Thirty! It *is*. Someone's messing about, commenting twice,' I said.

'Not necessarily,' said Mr Speed. 'Not if we count the entire class, pupils and teacher.'

'Did *you* put a comment, Mr Speed?'

'Now, you know perfectly well all contributions to the Worry Website are strictly confidential,' said Mr Speed.

I read them with great interest, trying to work out which was his.

I dream I've lost my old teddy Cuddle and I search everywhere and once I woke up and I still couldn't find him because he'd fallen out of bed and I cried.

I imagine Mr Speed crying for his teddy. Perhaps not.

I have awful nightmares too. Last night I dreamt about my mum and it should have been lovely but she turned into a wicked witch and cast a spell on me so I couldn't talk.

 I don't know if Mr Speed has still got a mum but I can't *ever* imagine him not talking, even in his dreams.

My biggest nightmare is dreaming that I'm with my dad and it's all happy, happy, happy at first but then he starts getting cross with me and my little brother and my mum so he storms

off and I wait and I wait but he doesn't come back.

That's quite definitely Samantha. So what did Mr

Speed put?

Aha!

I have this terrible nightmare that my feet develop throbbing bunions overnight and so I have to give up my brilliant career as a Premier-League footballer and retrain as a TEACHER!!!

I looked Mr Speed up and down.

'That's *your* nightmare, isn't it, Mr Speed?'

'The Worry Website insists on anonymity,' said Mr Speed.

'Yeah, but I *know* it's you! You weren't *really* a Premier-League footballer, were you?'

Mr Speed crumpled a piece of paper into a ball.

'Haven't you read about Speedy of United in all your football annuals?'

He dropped the paper ball and then aimed a nifty kick at it. Only it wasn't nifty. It wasn't even a kick. He missed it altogether.

I shook my head.

'You should have seen me *before* my bunions,' he said. 'So, Claire, we'll do a swapsie. You know my worst nightmare. Tell me yours.'

'Oh, it's – it's stupid,' I mumbled.

'But scary?'

'Very, very scary.'

Mr Speed looked at me carefully.

'You look like a little panda. Dark circles under the eyes. Are these nightmares so bad they stop you sleeping?'

'I don't *dare* sleep.'

Mr Speed raised his eyebrows.

'So tell me all about this nightmare. You can remember it?'

'I can't ever forget it,' I said. 'It's about this monster made out of green slime and—'

'Say no more!' said Mr Speed. 'I got the video out last week. Yep. It's seriously scary. Do Mum and Dad know you've watched it?'

'No!'

'Ah. I *see*!'

'You won't tell, will you, Mr Speed?'

'Let's see if we can radically edit your nightmare. Then we won't have to tell.'

'What do you mean? You can't edit nightmares. It just happens. And it's horrible.'

'I know it's horrible, Claire. But maybe you can control it, change it around a little bit. You've made it up inside your head, haven't you? It's like a story you've written in your sleep. OK, let's look on it as a first draft. Now you need to rewrite it. Change the scenario. You've got to get the better of this monster.'

'You mean flick my fingers and go zap and the Monster dies?' I said sarcastically. 'I don't think it would work.'

'No, probably not. It sounds a bit too powerful to be zapped into oblivion just like that. But you can be powerful too, Claire. What are your strengths, eh?'

I frowned at him.

'I'm good at football. But that's no use, not when it comes to the Monster.'

'Maybe it is. Kick a football at him. Aim right where it hurts. Make him double up.'

'Mr Speed, in the film the Monster defeats a whole *army*.'

'But this is the Monster in your head. He defeats whole armies, yes – but he's *very* wary of small girls with footballs.'

I thought Mr Speed was just being silly to cheer me up. He *did* make me feel a bit better when I was at school. But when I went home I started worrying again.

I got into bed with Judy and hung onto her tightly.

I tried very, very, very hard to stay awake – but eventually the duvet started turning slime green and I was dreaming and the Monster was there, oozing all over me.

I screamed and ran. The Monster was right behind me, reaching out, ready to slide his glistening tentacles round my neck. I tried running faster, speeding along. That made me think of Mr Speed. I looked down and there was a football at my feet. I was kicking it as I ran. I nudged it up into the air, caught hold of it, turned, and threw it right at the Monster's middle.

The ball got bigger. The Monster got smaller. Much, much smaller. It doubled up, wailing. It rocked itself, oozing lots of slime.

'There! That's shown you, you horrible Monster. Don't you dare come worrying me any more!'

The Monster groaned. It was shrinking rapidly now. It limped away, whimpering.

I kicked my football high in the air and then caught it in triumph . . .

'Ow! My head! Get *off*, Claire,' Judy yelled.

'Oops! Sorry. I thought it was a football,' I said, giggling.

'Look, get back to your *own* bed.'

'OK,' I said. I jumped out and climbed under my own duvet.

'You're all right, then?' Judy whispered. 'Look, come back with me if you get that nightmare again. Just don't bash me about the head again, OK?'

'I'm fine, Judy, really,' I said, yawning. 'Sh! Let's go to sleep now.'

I cuddled down under the duvet and slept properly. I didn't have the nightmare about the Monster. I had a funny dream about football. Mr Speed and I were on the same team. Mr Speed ran in a funny hobbly way because of his bunions but he managed to pass the ball to me – and I scored a brilliant goal.

WILLIAM'S WORRY

Type in your worry:

I am useless at everything.

That's it. And it is dead depressing to be me. I am William. I can't always spell it properly when I write in pencil. But it's OK on the computer because it does a wiggly red line under the word if you've spelt it wrong. Almost every word I tap out ends up with wiggly red lines.

I feel as if *I* am all wrong and there is a wiggly red line under me. You can change your spelling (though sometimes I have to try for *ages* and I have to ask someone helpful like Holly or Claire) but I can't change me. I wish I could.

I am bottom in the class. I am useless at everything. I can't add up or take away or multiply or divide. I can't make up stories. I can't remember History or Geography. I can't do IT. I can't draw.

I just do pin men. Sometimes I draw lots of pin men and they are all laughing at a stupid little pin boy.

My mum and dad don't laugh at me. My mum cries and my dad shouts. My brother says I am thick. He is younger than me but he's clever. His name is Richard. Sometimes Dad calls him Dick. He is definitely a Clever Dick.

Dad sometimes shortens my name too. He calls me Willie. They call me that at school sometimes too. It is *awful* having a name that sounds rude and makes people giggle.

Mr Speed called me Wee Willie Winkie today. I nearly cried.

'It's just a nursery rhyme, William,' said Mr Speed. 'Oh, don't look so stricken, lad. Here. You call *me* a silly name.'

I blinked at him.

'Go on, be a devil. Think up something really silly.'

I swallowed. 'Mr Silly Speed?' I said.

Mr Speed sighed. 'You're not over-endowed with imagination, are you, lad?'

I hung my head.

'Cheer up!' said Mr Speed. He ruffled my hair. 'There!' He wiped his fingers on my fringe. 'That's better. My fingers were very sticky.'

I felt my hair worriedly.

'I'm *joking*, William,' said Mr Speed.

The bell went for lunch. My tummy gave a loud rumble.

'If the bell electrics failed us, your stomach would act as a little alarm clock – *gurgle, gurgle* whenever it's lunchtime. What greater use is that?' said Mr Speed. 'I like a boy with a healthy appetite.'

I wasn't sure if he was joking or not. He seemed to

change his mind on dinner duty. It was fish fingers and baked beans and chips, and if you finish first you get seconds. So I went gobble, gobble and stood up quick, ready to dash back to the serving hatch.

'My goodness, William, take it easy!' said Mr Speed. 'Sit down and *chew*. You've got your entire plateful stuffed in your mouth! You'll choke to death, lad.'

'But – I – want – seconds – Mr – Speed!'

'William! Close your mouth! Good lord, lad, you're spraying half-masticated morsels all over us. Watch out, Samantha. We'll have to issue you with protective clothing if William carries on chomping with such abandon.'

I had to wait and chew until my mouth was empty. It wasn't *fair*. Half the other boys got to the hatch before me. Greg got the last portion of extra chips.

I looked at Mr Speed.

'Don't look so reproachful, lad, I can't stand it. OK, OK. My concerns for your digestion have done you out of a few chips—'

'A whole plateful, Mr Speed!'

'I haven't had *my* lunch yet. Stay behind and I dare say I'll donate a chip or two to you.'

He gave me *all* his chips – yummy, yummy, yummy!

'Slow down! You don't have to cram them all in together, William. I marvel at the capacity of that mouth of yours. Now, how are things at home, lad?'

I shrugged. I wouldn't have known what to say even if my mouth *wasn't* full of chips. I mean, home's *home*. What is there to say about it?

'Mum and Dad OK?'

'Mmm,' I said, swallowing.

'And how are you getting on with your brother?'

I didn't say anything but I must have pulled a face.

'That bad, eh?' said Mr Speed, laughing.

He lowered his voice. 'What about the little bed-wetting problem?'

I looked round nervously. Mr Speed had stopped everyone calling me Wetty Willie but I didn't want them *reminded*.

'It's heaps better, Mr Speed. Mum took me to the doctor, like you said, and I got this medicine.'

'Great! So things are looking up, William?'

'I suppose.'

'But you still feel a bit . . . useless?'

I stared at him. Mr Speed is magic. I wondered

how on earth he knew. He could have read it on the Worry Website but you're not allowed to sign your name so he couldn't possibly work out it was *me*.

'You're not useless, William.'

'I *am*, Mr Speed.'

'No, no, no, William.'

'Yes, yes, yes, Mr Speed. I can't do *nothing*.'

'Anything. And you *can*.' Mr Speed screwed up his face. 'You're very good at . . .'

I waited.

'You're a very good boy, full stop,' said Mr Speed.

'But I wish I could be good *at* something, Mr Speed,' I said.

'Well, perhaps we can give you a bit of extra help with your school work?'

I must have pulled another face.

'Don't look so appalled! OK, OK, we'll try another tack. What about games? We could maybe get Claire to help you with your footie skills.'

'I'm useless at football, Mr Speed. I always trip myself up when I try to kick the ball.'

'Look, lad, we're not trying to turn you into David Beckham.'

'I had a David Beckham haircut in the holidays. My dad said it would make me look tough. But it didn't work.'

'Never you mind, William,' said Mr Speed. 'We'll

make *something* work for you, just you wait and see. Things are going to start looking up for you, lad.'

So I waited. Nothing much happened in the afternoon. I came bottom in the spelling test. I painted a snail picture all different colours in Art. I used too much water and the blue ran into the yellow and  the red dribbled all down the page so that it looked as if my snail had had a nasty accident.

My mum got mad at me for getting paint all over my school trousers. Richard and I got into a fight  over which of us owned a blue biro. I *know* it was my biro. But Richard won. So I couldn't do my homework as I didn't have anything to write with. Then Dad came home and Richard and I played catch with him in the garden. Well, Dad and Richard played catch. I played drop.

Then we had spag bol for tea (I'm not even going to *try* to spell it all out). It was hotter than I thought so I had to spit my first mouthful out. Mum thumped me and Dad shouted at me for crying and Richard laughed at me for being a baby.

I went to bed. And don't tell anyone but I wet myself because I forgot to take my special medicine.

Things haven't looked up *yet*.

When I got to school I looked at the Worry Website to see if I'd got any comments.

I'm sure you're not useless at everything.

Don't worry, I'm pretty useless at everything too.

I bet you're useFUL, not useLESS.

Things started to look up quite a bit. I felt so pleased that people didn't seem to think I was useless after all. Though of course they didn't know it was me. Perhaps if I'd put my name they'd have said I was ultra-ultra-ultra-useless. Especially as I can't always spell my name right.

We had another spelling test which was a bit of a nasty surprise as we only usually have one a week.

'Don't look so down-hearted, children. There are going to be two special prizes to spur you on. Two of my very special pens, no less.'

Mr Speed produced a pen from each pocket like a cowboy whipping out two guns. Mr Speed's pens *are* special. They are black and they write with a very fine line. They make the worst handwriting in the

76

world look much neater. Mr Speed goes crazy if any of us borrow his special pens. But now he was giving away *two* as prizes – and it wasn't even the end of term.

I wished I was good at spelling. But I am such rubbish at spelling I knew it was absolutely no use hoping to win a pen.

'I want you all to try very hard,' said Mr Speed, and then he started saying all these words.

There was a lot of sighing and muttering and nibbling of pens. Some of the class whispered.

'I want absolutely *no* conferring,' said Mr Speed.

Nobody tried to confer with me anyway. Which is not surprising. I can't even *spell* surprising.

Mr Speed told us to have a go at spelling everything, so I did. Even the very, very hard words. I'm not going to write them here – I'll never get them right.

I did lots and lots of crossings out. So many that my paper tore. But it didn't really matter. I knew I wasn't going to do well in the spelling test. I knew I was going to do really, really badly.

I was right. We had to swap papers. Lisa marked mine and I marked hers. Lisa is clever. She got fourteen out of twenty. She is also kind. I didn't

get *any* of my spellings right. She put up her hand to talk to Mr Speed.

'William's very nearly spelt "naughty" right, Mr Speed. And his "because" has only got one mistake. So could he have a half each for those?'

'Absolutely not,' said Mr Speed. 'A word is either spelt correctly or it isn't. And William's *isn't*.'

'But that's not very fair, Mr Speed,' said Lisa.

'Life isn't fair, Lisa,' said Mr Speed gently.

I hoped Lisa might win one of Mr Speed's pens but Holly got *eighteen* spellings completely correct. She was dead chuffed to win the pen, especially as her little

sister Hannah had leant too hard on Holly's old pen and made it go all splodgy.

'Maybe you'll win the second pen, Lisa,' I said hopefully.

But Samantha got sixteen spellings absolutely ace-standard correct. She batted her big blue eyes, looking very, very hopeful.

'Now we have the *second* prize-winner,' said Mr Speed. Strangely, he wasn't looking at Samantha. He was looking at *me*!

'This goes to the child who has had the sheer

dogged temerity to resist all my persuasive teaching skills and persists in being a truly inventively gargantuan appalling speller.'

I gaped at Mr Speed. I hadn't understood a word he was saying. But I understood the *next* bit.

'The second pen is awarded to the child who has the *most* spelling mistakes. Step forward, William!'

So *I* got the second prize pen. Some of the children groaned and said it wasn't fair – but most of them clapped. Greg even *cheered*!

I felt very, very, very pleased.

I didn't feel exactly *proud* though. I am a bit thick but I'm not completely stupid. I knew it was just a booby prize. It's not the same getting a prize for being the worst at something. I still wished I could be the *best* at something so I wouldn't feel quite so useless.

Mr Speed always makes up a story for us after spelling. He uses every single spelling word within the story. It was one of his *When I was a little boy* stories. He told us his accommodation was a miniature but pleasant house and his parents paid him every attention even though it was occasionally necessary to discipline him because he was so naughty. He enjoyed eating delicious breakfasts, especially sausages. He ate his substantial sausages with such determined commitment that he invariably made himself physically sick but this was a penalty he bore with relative indifference. His sausage consumption was brilliant training for the daily Enormous Mouthful contest that took place at lunchtime.

Mr Speed wanted to stop his story then and there because he'd used up all the hard spelling words but we all complained and said, 'No, Mr Speed, go on, tell us more,' because we all wanted to hear about the Enormous Mouthful contest.

'You mean I've never told you about the Enormous Mouthful contest?' said Mr Speed, looking astonished. 'Well, maybe it's just as well. If I tell you about it you'll only start up something similar yourselves.'

'No we won't, Mr Speed,' we all chorused.

'Oh yes you will!'

'Oh no we won't!'

We went on like this, getting louder, Mr Speed conducting us with his arms. Then he quickly put his finger to

his lips and we all *whispered* – even me. This is a game we play when Mr Speed is in a good mood.

Then he told us all about the food they had for school dinners when he was a little boy. You couldn't choose in those long ago days. You never ever had chips (my favourites). You had disgusting things like smelly stew all glistening with fat and grey mince that looked as if someone had chewed it all up. You had cabbage like old seaweed and lumpy mashed potato and tinned peas that smelt like feet.

'But we ate it all up because if you didn't you weren't allowed to have pudding. Puddings were the whole *point* of school dinners. We had jam roly-poly and bread-and-butter pudding and chocolate sponge with chocolate sauce and apple pie and custard and absolute best of all, trifle. There were also a lot of boring puddings like rice and semolina and something particularly revolting called tapioca that looked like frog spawn – but even these were palatable because we were given spoonfuls of jam or brown sugar or raisins. Those of us who were particularly greedy wangled *two* spoonfuls. These were to be savoured. However, the milk puddings needed to be golloped down as quickly as possible because they were so horrible. *That* was the start of the Enormous Mouthful club. Someone got hold of a big serving spoon and we had this ridiculous contest to see who could swallow the largest mouthful.'

'Did you win, Mr Speed?'

'Do you think I would have been such a rude and ill-mannered and mischievous child as to take part in such an indigestion-inducing eating contest?' said Mr Speed.

'YES!' we yelled.

Mr Speed grinned and bowed. 'You know me well, my children. Yes, I took part. Yes, I choked and spluttered and snorted and got violent hiccups. And *yes*, I won the Enormous Mouthful contest.' Mr Speed paused. 'But you children are strictly forbidden to take part in any similar contest. Do you all hear me?'

'Yes, Mr Speed,' we said.

'And to hear . . . ?'

'Is to obey,' we chorused.

We heard all right. But of course we didn't obey. We had our very own Enormous Mouthful contest at lunchtime. It was not quite as easy for us. We didn't have milk puddings which are

soft and slippy. We have bulky, crunchy, crispy food that won't go with one swallow. We had to experiment and do an awful lot of chewing (and a little choking too).

Chips proved to be the easiest food for the Enormous Mouthful contest. My favourite.

I shovelled up an entire plateful of chips and crammed them all into my mouth and I WON the Enormous Mouthful contest!

I came FIRST.

So I'm not useless. I'm the champion Enormous Mouthful Eater of all time. Whoopee! Whoopee! Whoopee!

Mr Speed was right. Things have looked up *enormously*.

SAMANTHA'S WORRY

Type in your worry:

I miss my dad. It's just not the same now he's gone. And my mum is either sad or snappy nowadays. And my little brother is ever so naughty and keeps spoiling all my things. And no-one wants to be my boyfriend. And I don't think my teacher likes me any more either. He always used to pick me to be his special messenger but now he picks Holly. Or Greg. Or Claire. Or even William.

It's so awful. I've always been the girl everyone *likes*. Everyone always wants to sit next to me or be my partner. Everyone wants to be invited for tea at my house or come to my party.

But now it's all changed.

Dad went last year. He and Mum had lots of rows but everyone's parents have rows. I didn't *like* it but it didn't really bother me. My little brother Simon  used to crawl into my bed and sit on my lap and he made me cup my hands over his funny little sticky-out ears so he couldn't hear the shouting.

I didn't have anyone to put their hands over my ears but I didn't mind too much. I wanted to know what was going on. I was always on Dad's side no matter what. I love my mum but she's not *Dad*. Dad looks like a film star, he really does, with lovely blond hair and deep blue eyes and he's really fit  too because he works out and plays a lot of sport. That was what Mum and Dad rowed about. Dad always flirted with all the ladies he met at badminton and tennis and swimming. My mum used to go too but then she had me and couldn't get out so much and then she had Simon and stayed a bit plump so she didn't want to wear tight sporty clothes anyway.

Dad took me sometimes. He got me my own special little tennis racket and threw the ball at me again and again. We went swimming on Sunday mornings and he showed me how to dive and swim right down to the bottom of the deep end and he called me his little dolphin.

But then he met this horrible woman, Sandy, at his gym and Mum found out. Dad didn't stop seeing Sandy. He packed his bag and walked out and stopped seeing *us*.

He said he wasn't leaving me, he was just leaving Mum. He said he was still my dad and he loved me lots and lots and lots and he'd see me every single week. But that hasn't worked out because he and Sandy have moved away and now that Sandy's going to have a baby, Dad doesn't come over so much. I haven't seen him for weeks now. He was supposed to come last weekend for Simon's birthday, he absolutely *promised*, but the day before he rang to say Sandy had got these special tickets for a trip to Paris as a surprise so they were going there instead.

Mum shouted down the phone that he obviously

couldn't care less about his own son and his birthday. Dad said that he loved Simon very much but perhaps it wasn't good for him to see him so often anyway because Simon got very over-excited and silly and the visits were obviously upsetting him.

Simon kicked Sandy hard on the shin the last time we went round to Dad's new place.

I wished I was young enough to kick Sandy too.

Mum said we didn't *need* Dad at Simon's party, we'd have a much better time by ourselves. But we didn't.

I don't suppose Dad will come to my party now either. No-one will come to my party. No-one likes me any more. It was so awful on the bus when we all went to the museum. Greg was horrible to me. I thought he really *liked* me.

But he's nuts on Holly instead. Holly hates me too. She always pulls a face and sighs when I start talking. And Mr Speed likes Holly best now, I just know he does. He's always chatting to her. He makes a great big fuss of Claire too. And though he's always telling Greg off you can tell he thinks he's really funny. Mr Speed even likes silly-willy William more than me.

William banged right into me at lunchtime and spilt his orange squash all down my school blouse. I shouted at him. William looked upset in his silly, goofy way.

'I'm sorry, Samantha. I didn't *mean* to. I was just in a hurry to get seconds.'

 'Look at my blouse! It's all *orange*,' I said, plucking at my dripping blouse.

'It looks like a pretty pattern. Orange is a lovely colour,' said William. 'Here, let's dry it a bit.'

He picked up the messy old cloth we use to wipe the tables and started dabbing at me, smearing bits of old chip and pizza sauce all over my blouse, making it a hundred times worse.

'Leave *off*, William. Don't be so *stupid*,' I shouted.

William burst into tears like a baby. Mr Speed came dashing up.

'Hey hey hey! Why are two of my favourite pupils

abusing each other so bitterly?' he
asked. 'Don't *cry*, William.'

'I'm not *anyone's* favourite,' I said,
and I burst into tears too.

Mr Speed tutted and sighed
and mopped us both. He told
William he could have extra
chips if he stopped crying.
William cheered up immediately
and went bounding off.

'I think your problems are possibly less easily
solved, Samantha,' said Mr Speed. 'But you'll
certainly feel a *little* better if we find you a change of
blouse. That one's sopping. How about changing
into your PE shirt?'

'I took it home for Mum to wash,' I sniffed.

'Oh dear, oh dear. Never mind. Come with me.'

I trailed after him miserably.

'I might have someone's spare PE top in the
classroom cupboard,' said Mr Speed.

While he was searching high and low amongst
ancient confiscated Pokémon cards and single
plimsolls and dried-up felt tips I went and looked to
see if I had any replies on the Worry Website.

Comments:

My dad is so scary I wish he WASN'T at home with us.

My dad's great but he's always tired because of his new

89

job so I hardly ever get to talk to him either.

My mum gets cross too. AND my dad.

Yeah, and MY little sister can be a right pain too, and as a matter of fact I don't see my mum but I don't go on and on about it. And I can't help it if Mr Speed sometimes picks me to do stuff now. It doesn't mean he's stopped liking you.

Mr Speed came and peered over my shoulder.

'Budge over, Samantha.'

He typed:

Of course your teacher likes you. He is a wonderful, kindly man who likes everyone. ESPECIALLY sad little souls going through a bad patch.

'There!' said Mr Speed. 'Do you think this particular sad little soul will be comforted, Samantha?'

'Maybe just a little bit,' I said.

'It's probably surprising to an extremely popular girl like you that someone can feel so lonely,' said Mr Speed.

'Mmm!' I said.

'I can't find a spare shirt anywhere. Come with me. We'll see if Mrs Holmes has a hidden cache in her office.'

We went down the corridor to the main entrance. Mr Speed bobbed into the Secretary's office while I hung around, picking at my sticky sodden blouse. There were paintings stuck all over the walls. Some of them had been there a while and were curling at the edges. There were a few *My Family* paintings our class did last year.

My picture was there. I'd painted my dad and my mum and my little brother and me, all of us standing in a line and smiling. The red paint had run a bit when I did my face, so my lips were huge.

I stared at my stupid gigantic grin and then I punched the paper, bashing my own pinkly-painted face. My little brother was grinning too. It was his fault Dad didn't come any more, because he behaved so badly. I hit my little brother too. The paper tore a little, so that my mum's head was nearly split in two. I didn't care. If she hadn't shouted so much Dad might have stayed.

I looked at Dad. I'd painted him extra carefully, though I couldn't get the colours quite right. His hair was bright lemon, his eyes ultramarine, his cheeks scarlet. I wasn't really that great at painting. I couldn't make my dad look handsome enough.

I'd printed MY FAMILY underneath. But Dad wasn't really part of our family any more. He was part of a brand-new family with Sandy. He was going to have this new baby too. I hoped it wouldn't be a little girl. He'd love her much more than he loved me.

My fist clenched and I punched Dad hard, again and again, harder and harder.

'Hey, hey! Stop it! Samantha, you'll hurt your poor hand,' Mr Speed shouted, rushing out of Mrs Holmes's office.

'I don't care,' I yelled. I punched my painting again, even though there were beads of blood on my knuckles and my arm throbbed all the way up past my elbow.

'Well, *I* care,' said Mr Speed. 'Good lord, child, *stop* it.'

He caught hold of my hand. I burst into tears. Mr Speed patted me gently on the back and then led me into Mrs Holmes's office. She found me a box of tissues, a clean blouse and a big bandage for my fist.

Mr Speed came back to collect me. 'Ah! All mopped up?'

I nodded.

'I'll take you back to the classroom, sweetheart.

Dear, oh dear. I'd better have a word with your mum when she comes to collect you.'

'I don't want you to have a word with my mum, Mr Speed. I want you to have a word with my *dad*.' I looked up at him. 'You're great at fixing things, aren't you? I bet you could sort out all the worries on our website. Well, why can't you sort out mine? Can't you make my dad come back?'

Mr Speed sighed.

'I can't do that, Samantha. I can sometimes solve little tiny problems but I can't do a thing about big sad problems. Not even mine. My own marriage broke up a while ago. I know just how you're feeling, poppet.'

'Did you leave your children, Mr Speed?'

'I don't have any children,' he said. He gave a funny little grin. 'Maybe teaching all you lot put me off having any of my own?'

'But if you *did* have children would you walk out on them?'

'Oh, Samantha, how can I possibly answer that one?' said Mr Speed.

'I bet you wouldn't,' I said. I thought about my dad. I saw him walking off, his arm round Sandy. I stood still in the corridor. 'I hate my dad,' I whispered. The words tasted bad in my mouth so I

spat them out louder. *'I hate my dad!'*

'Yes. I can understand that,' said Mr Speed. 'Though you still love him lots too. But you're very, very angry with him. That's why you started punching his picture. But that's not really a good idea, is it? You only hurt your poor old hand.' He carefully patted my bandage.

'What do you think I should do then, Mr Speed? Punch my *dad*?'

'That's maybe not a good idea either.'

'Our Simon kicked his girlfriend. She got a big bruise on her leg.'

'Oh dear. I shall wear shinpads when your Simon comes up into the Juniors. He's in Miss Morgan's class, isn't he? She'll channel all his energy into finger painting or digging in the sandpit. Excellent activities! How about a spot of digging, Samantha? How about getting a spade and having a good dig in your garden whenever you feel especially cross or miserable?'

'We live in a flat, Mr Speed. We haven't even got a window box.'

'Ah. Well . . . perhaps we could purloin a little patch of the school garden?' Mr Speed smiled. 'Let's go and have a look round, see if we can find the right little corner.'

So Mr Speed and I went across the playground

over to the garden. I'd played on the grass heaps of times but I'd never really looked properly at the garden bit before. I peered at the plants. Mr Speed started spouting all these long Latin names. I listened politely, not really taking any of it in until Mr Speed pointed to a patch of earth behind a big bush.

'Aha! This looks the perfect plot. OK, Samantha. This is your patch. I'll find you a spade. You can dig here any playtime or lunchtime, before school, after school, whenever.'

I tried having a little dig there and then. I couldn't do too much because of my sore hand. I wasn't very good at it at first. I was too quick and clumsy and couldn't budge the hard earth. Mr Speed showed me how to do it slowly and rhythmically, putting my foot on the spade, straightening up so I wouldn't hurt my back.

'That's it! Ah, you've got into the swing of things now. We'll be hiring you out on building sites at this rate. You'll have muscles like Madonna by the end of the month.'

I think digging *has* made me stronger. Greg was mucking

around in the corridor doing a silly dance and showing off in front of Holly. He did a twiddly bit and banged right into me. I pushed him away so hard he nearly fell over! That'll teach him. I can't stick Greg now. I don't envy Holly one bit. I wouldn't want him as a boyfriend if you paid me.

I don't want *William* as my boyfriend either. But he seems to think he is!

I cheered up a bit after I had my first little dig. I felt mean for making William cry so I went up to him after school. He cowered away as if I was going to hit him. That made me feel worse – so I put my arm round him.

'Sorry I yelled at you, William,' I said, and I gave him a hug.

I thought that was it. It *was* as far as I was concerned. But now William goes pink whenever I go near him and he follows me around like a little dog. He tries to carry my schoolbag and rushes to get my school lunch for me and whenever I go for a dig William trails after me and wants to dig too.

I had a little moan about it to Mr Speed.

'It was *my* private patch, Mr Speed, and now William wants to dig too.'

'Yeah, I can see it's annoying having young William under your feet all the time, Samantha. But on the other hand he needs a bit of digging therapy himself.'

'OK, Mr Speed. But I wish he didn't have to dig on *my* bit. I tried planting an apple core just to see if it might just grow up into an apple tree and William dug it up the very next day.'

'Perhaps you could mark off your special bit and make sure William keeps to his? And I'll let you have a few seeds and bulbs if you fancy a spot of real gardening. That's a great idea.'

So I divided my patch into two and told William he could dig all he wanted on his own bit. Mr Speed brought us lots of lovely things to plant in our new gardens. Mine were a mixture of pretty flower seeds: pinks and pansies, primroses and sweet peas.

'And I'll see if I can get some raspberry canes too. They'll be a lot speedier than apple trees,' said Mr Speed. 'I thought you'd like to grow something to eat too, William, seeing as you're the lad of gargantuan appetite. I thought potatoes would be more in your line.

Think of all those chips! And we might go for something really exotic like a marrow. That *would* be a challenge for the Enormous Mouthful contest! But you'd better have a few flowers too.'

Mr Speed handed him a seed packet with a picture of deep purply-red-and-white little flowers on it. They were called Sweet Williams!

'I wish there was a flower called Sweet Samantha,' said Mr Speed.

So now I've stopped digging and started gardening. Little weeny green shoots are starting to grow through the very well-dug earth. They might just be little weeds though. We'll have to wait and see.

Mr Speed brought William and me a tomato plant today. My dad loves tomatoes. He can gollop up a whole pound, easy-peasy. If he comes to visit when my tomatoes

are ripe I might offer him his very own home-grown tomato salad. But if he *doesn't* come then Mum and

Simon and me will eat them all up. Well, I'll save enough for a special tomato sandwich for Mr Speed.

I have one worry less. My teacher really *does* like me lots!

The first Worry Website story about Holly was made available on the Internet last year by BOL and the Guardian. I suggested we have a competition to see if any children wanted to make up their own story about a child in Mr Speed's class who has a worry to type onto the website. I was delighted that there were 15,000 entries. The shortlisted stories I personally judged were all of such a high standard that it was agonizing only being able to choose one. But that one story was so special that it simply had to be the winner. It's by Lauren Roberts, aged twelve.

I'd planned to make Lauren's the last story in the book but it ends so sadly that I decided to add one more story myself, just to try to end things on a happy note.

So here is Lauren's wonderful prize-winning Worry Website story.

Jacqueline Wilson

LISA'S WORRY

Type in your worry:

I . . .

I think . . .

Oh, this is useless. I could type in a thousand
worries if I had to, but I can't find one un-stupid
enough to put in. I do that. Make up words from
somewhere. I make lots of things up, fantasy things,
like creatures and magical people so I can disappear
into my own world whenever I like.

I don't need to disappear anywhere at home though;
I've got my mum. She's the best mum in the world.

Sometimes I draw her with flowing black hair and piercing blue eyes, trapped in a tower waiting for a prince to come and rescue her. My mum is beautiful, and she's trapped. Stuck in a flat with me and the wicked wizard who spends all our money on beer and cigarettes.

The wicked wizard is my dad. We only see him at teatime and in the morning now. He's out all night at the pub. My mum keeps saying that he'll change. He never will.

I remember when I was little, and we all used to sit on their big bed and he used to read to me. My favourite was *The Ugly Duckling*. I can remember my mum reading the swan's parts in a smooth soft voice, and Dad doing the ugly duckling and the ducks' parts in funny high-pitched voices that made me giggle. I loved that room. It had a nice musky smell. We  had to move when I was seven because Dad got a new job. That's when he started changing.

He was always late home, and then he went straight

to bed. He stopped playing games with me and Mum. He didn't talk any more, only shouted.

I missed my old school and my best friend, Sarah. We used to be inseparable. The teachers would rush up to us before breaktimes and ask us to keep the Reception classes under control, because we were one-hundred-per-cent reliable. We kept them occupied by doing this little comedy routine. Their favourite was the 'she's behind you' routine. Sarah stood in front and said, 'I wonder where Lisa could be' – and just then I'd run past behind her and pull funny faces. The classes would all point and shout, 'She's behind you!' Then I'd hide again. They loved that.

When I came to my new school I didn't fit in. Some of the girls tried to talk to me but I wouldn't talk to them. I really wanted to make some friends but whenever someone talked to me I remembered Sarah and felt guilty.

The boys ignored me until we did football in PE (girls v boys) and we won 6–3. I scored five goals. Then all the boys picked me for their footie team, and reckoned I was dead sporty. They picked me for other

teams, like rounders and basketball, but soon I realized I couldn't hit a rounders ball with a bat the size of Calcutta and I couldn't score a basket if they paid me.

Mrs Bryn shouted at me a lot for being behind in class and not doing homework. I was glad to move up to Mr Speed's class.

Mr Speed was great at cheering me up. He helped me catch up with my work and make friends. It felt great.

But one day after I'd been to Claire's house, I came home and my mum was crying. She said that she'd just banged her arm and bruised it. I hugged her tight and told her she'd be all right. She had hurt her face too, but it didn't cross my mind what might be going on until I went to bed. It was just as I fell asleep that I understood that my dad – the same squeaky duckling, imaginary games, laughing, smiling dad that I had loved with all my heart right up until the point he changed – could be hurting my mother.

I was afraid to leave my mum in the morning, so I started coughing like crazy, and she tucked me up on the sofa. I pretended to be asleep and heard my dad shouting and my mum trying not to let him wake me, which made him shout more.

I opened my eyes in time to see him hit Mum and leave. My body froze. As soon as the door closed I rushed to my mum's side.

The next day when he came back he was all lovey-dovey, looking for forgiveness. I expected Mum to turn him right away, but she let him in! He still lives with us, and he's being nice so far. He'll snap any second now.

Type in your worry:

I'm starting to get spots.

After all, there are some things you don't want people to know.

NATASHA'S WORRY

Type in your worry:

I wish I could take part in the concert.

Mr Speed is organizing a concert. The whole class keeps going on about it. William is fussing because he can't do anything. Everyone else is singing or playing a musical instrument or reciting a poem or dancing. I can't sing or play or recite or dance. But people don't expect me to be able to perform. I can't even walk or talk. But it's OK. I manage. I use a wheelchair. It's electric and powerful so sometimes I can muck about chasing

106

the other kids. I have a special speaking machine too. My fingers work in a shaky sort of way so I can press the right button and words get said. Not always the words I *want*. I can't say *rude* words when I'm cross unless I spell them out laboriously. I usually choose to say short easy words because it's so much quicker.

It makes me sound a bit simple. I know I look it. But I'm NOT. I go to a special school but we have proper lessons, Maths and English and Science and stuff just like everyone else. And one day a week I go up the road and round the corner to Mapleton Juniors to see what it's like in an ordinary classroom.

Only it's not the slightest *bit* ordinary. They have this really wacky teacher Mr Speed. I wasn't sure I liked him at first. He leaps about a lot and shouts and uses weird long words. The teachers and helpers at my special school walk carefully and talk quietly and use words everyone can understand. I got a bit nervous when he came near me at first. My arms jerked about more than usual and I shrank down even smaller than usual. Most people think I'm younger than I am because I'm quite little. They treat you like a baby anyway if you use a wheelchair.

But not Mr Speed.

'Hello, Natasha,' he said, straight to me. Lots of people look at Wendy, my helper, even though they're talking to me.

I made my machine say hello back. Mr Speed told the class about my talking machine and asked if I'd say hello to them too. I did. Then I added, 'Let's make friends.' This was artful. I knew they'd all go, 'Aaah!' and say yes. You need to get children on your side. Sometimes they can be *sooo* mean. They can call you Spaz and Dummy and the Veggie. You can't have thin skin if you have a disability. Sometimes I've had to have skin like a *rhinoceros* to stop all the rude remarks hurting me.

But Mr Speed's class were all good to me right from the start. Almost *too* nice. The girls begged Wendy to let them push me around and they treated me like a doll, fussing with my hair and fiddling with my chair strap and speaking very loud and very s–l–o–w–l–y. The boys waved at me a bit nervously, keeping well clear of my wheelchair – in case I leapt up and bit them? They were all ever so polite though – apart from William. He didn't mean to be rude. He isn't that sort of kid. He just stared and stared and stared at me, as if I was an extraordinary television programme. The pretty girl, Samantha, gave him a little nudge and whispered to him not to stare so.

'Why?' said William.

'Because it's rude,' Samantha hissed.

'But she looks so *funny*,' said William.

'Sh!' said Samantha, going pink.

'She can't hear, can she?' said William. 'She can't *speak*.'

It seems to me that it's old William who has the disability – a *mental* one. But I suppose he can't help it. Same as I can't help looking funny. William's right about that. My mum says I've got a lovely smile and my dad says I'm his Pretty Princess and Wendy says I've got beautiful blue eyes – but they are simply being kind. Mr Speed says I have lovely long hair. He gently pulls my plaits and calls me Rapunzel. I quite like this. I like my hair too. But I know pretty hair doesn't stop me looking weird. Well, not unless I turned into a real Rapunzel and grew it down to my ankles and covered myself with it, like a great furry hood and coat.

I'd like that. I could stay hidden inside. You're always so *obvious* if you have a disability. You can't hide behind the other kids or creep to a corner of the classroom. You're always on display in your big wheelchair, often with your helper beside you. You can't whisper secrets when you have a voice machine. You can't *have* secrets.

I had to get Wendy to tap in my worry on the website as I can't reach the computer keys properly. And when I wanted to look at the replies I couldn't just wait for an appropriate moment and nip across and have a quick glance. I had to get Wendy to manoeuvre my wheelchair in and out the desks and then click on all the right places on the screen.

I waited until after school when everyone had gone home. Mr Speed was still there, but he pretended not to notice what Wendy and I were doing. He was trying to construct some kind of fairy-tale carriage out of cardboard boxes for the concert. He was doing his best with gold

paint and old pram wheels but the audience might have to be kind and use their imagination. A girl called Lisa was painting scenery in a corner. She nodded to me shyly and then went on with her work. She seemed much more artistic than Mr Speed. She'd painted an all-purpose fairy-tale land with princesses with long golden hair and pink enchanted castles and wicked wizards swigging from their own bubbling cauldrons.

That's another thing I can't do. Paint. I know exactly how I want to do it in my head but it won't come out like that on the page. My hand just jerks and it all splodges. I won't even try now.

Mr Speed saw me staring at Lisa's scenery.

'It's good, isn't it, Natasha?'

'Very, very, very good,' I said with my voice machine. Wendy thought my finger had gone into spasm by the third 'very' and went to help me. I shook my head at her impatiently. Then I felt mean. It is so hard to have a helper all the time when you don't *want* to be helped.

Lisa looked up and smiled.

'Thank you,' she muttered, and carried on.

'The class members who lack specific talents are all in this mini-pantomime at the end of the concert.

That's what all this scenery is for. Oh lordy, this *wretched* concert,' said Mr Speed. He pressed down too hard on his fairy carriage and it collapsed. Mr Speed said a very rude word and then put his hand over his mouth. 'I hope you girls didn't hear that,' he said.

Lisa giggled. I giggled. Wendy giggled too.

'Why do I get involved year after year?' said Mr Speed. 'It's just one big worry.'

'Type your worry into the website!' I spoke slowly.

Mr Speed waited patiently and laughed when I was finished. 'Teachers aren't allowed to have worries,' he said.

He glanced ever so casually at the screen.

'What sort of comments has the latest worry attracted? I believe someone wants to be in the concert?'

'You know the someone is me,' I said.

'You're not daft, are you, Natasha?' said Mr Speed.

William *is* daft. He had typed in:

Why cant you bee in the consat? I am in it and I am useless at sining and dansing and stuff. But I am dooing cungring triks.

I blinked.

'What?'

'I think the lad means "conjuring",' said Mr Speed.

'I've helped him work out a routine with young Samantha.'

I blinked again.

'Can William *do* conjuring tricks?' Wendy asked doubtfully. She hasn't got to know all the children in Mr Speed's class – but you can't miss William.

'No, of course he can't. He drops all the cards and fails to pull out the ribbons and he can't produce the toy white rabbit from his cardboard top hat,' said Mr Speed, chuckling.

I decided maybe I didn't like Mr Speed after all.

'They will laugh at him,' I said. I can't put expression into my voice machine, but I tried to look disapproving.

'Don't frown at me, madam. They're *supposed* to laugh. William is *deliberately* mucking up his act. He's playing a totally useless conjuror. Well, he doesn't need to try hard, does he? And Samantha is going to get all gussied up in her ballet frock, being his beautiful blond assistant, and *she* will sort him out and do the trick each time.'

I nodded. I looked at another comment on the computer screen.

I wanted to sing a song with Holly but she's doing a dance with her little sister so I've got to sing on my own and my voice goes all wobbly and Mr Speed shouts, 'You're out of tune, lad' and makes it worse so I don't want to be in the concert.

'Oh dear,' said Mr Speed, reading over my shoulder. 'I do sound a bully, don't I? I'm not really that bad, am I, Natasha?'

'Yes!' I said.

Mr Speed laughed. Wendy laughed. Lisa looked up from her painting and laughed. I laughed too.

'Is everyone taking part in the concert?' Wendy asked.

'Not quite everyone. Lisa says she doesn't feel like performing. She's come to my rescue with the scenery. And hopefully she might help out with the props too.' Mr Speed gestured at the remains of his fairy carriage.

I asked Wendy to wheel me over to Lisa so I could have a closer look at her scenery. She parked me beside her and then went to have a little talk with Mr Speed. Probably about me. People are always having little talks about me and my progress – or lack of it. I'm OK at the difficult stuff. Ten out of ten in all lessons. I'm just useless at all the easy-peasy ordinary things everyone else takes for granted. I'm trapped in my baby body, unable to do anything for myself. Nought out of ten for walking, talking, going to the loo, combing my hair, whatever.

I like the way Lisa has her hair, short and spiky. It

looks seriously cool. Maybe it's time I had *my* hair cut?

I started telling her with my machine that I liked her hair. The mechanical voice made her jump and she blotched a bit of paint so that her princess got a red spot on the end of her nose to match her scarlet smile.

'Whoops!'

'Sorry I've spoilt your lady.' I wanted to say I'm sorry my mechanical voice sounds so stupid and I loved the way she's painted the beautiful fairy-tale princess but it would have taken too long.

'I think the wizard's put a curse on her. She's got spots. So have I, actually,' said Lisa. 'My mum says it's too much chocolate.'

My hand wasn't behaving itself because I wanted to make friends with Lisa so much. I had to make several stabs at it before I managed to say, 'I love chocolate.'

'I've got a Galaxy here,' said Lisa, fishing it out of her pocket with painty fingers. 'Do you want a bite?' Then she went pink. 'I mean . . . can you . . . can you eat, like, normally?'

'Try me!' I said.

She had the sense to break off a small square. She held it tentatively to my mouth. I tried *sooo* hard not to drool on her. I sucked the chocolate in and as I

 munched I made my voice machine say, 'I can talk with my mouth full.'

Lisa burst out laughing and gave me another piece of chocolate. She ate a square herself and then started sketching a house in a little wood at the right of her scenery.

'This is going to be the witch's gingerbread house, right? It's made out of sweets and chocolate and cakes and cookies. Maybe I could do it a bit like a collage, eh? Stick real little bits of chocolate on the roof?'

'Fruit gums for stained-glass windows and marshmallows for window ledges and Toblerone for a gable,' I spelt out endlessly. It took for ever but Lisa nodded at each word and calmly went on painting.

'That's so great, Natasha. If only you could paint too. What if we strapped a brush to your hand?'

'Too shaky.'

'How about your mouth?' Lisa gently put the end of her paintbrush in my mouth and then tried to push me nearer the desk where a piece of paper was set out. I saw Wendy step forward to help with the wheelchair but Mr Speed stopped her.

I tried hard, clenching my teeth. I know lots of people with severe disabilities use their mouths. Some really little kids at my special school can operate anything with a wriggle of their lips. But I find it incredibly difficult. It took me years to learn to drink with a *straw*, for goodness' sake. I'm hardly going to paint Mona Lisas with my mouth.

I had several goes but I kept dropping the stupid brush the minute it touched the paper. I thought Lisa would quickly get fed up with this lark but she was incredibly patient. I was the one who spat the brush out deliberately in disgust.

'Try again, Natasha,' said Mr Speed.

I *knew* he'd been watching us.

'You try,' I said with my machine. You can get away with being a bit cheeky when you've got disabilities.

'OK, I'll have a go,' said Mr Speed.

He sat in front of the piece of paper, stuck a paintbrush in his mouth, dabbled it – with difficulty – in a pot of pink paint and then tried to paint with it. He was too  jerky and the paint much too runny. It spattered everywhere. Wendy was standing too near.

117

A spray landed on her nose, like pink freckles. Lisa and I fell about laughing. I almost did it literally, flopping sideways in my chair. Wendy was a good sport, laughing too as she hauled me upright.

''Orry, 'orry,' Mr Speed mumbled, his mouth still full of paintbrush. He had another go, frowning ferociously with concentration. He kept blotching, but by his fifth piece of paper he'd managed a lopsided daisy.

He removed the paintbrush and flourished his painting. Lisa and Wendy clapped and I pressed 'well done' on my talk machine. Mr Speed presented the painting to Wendy apologizing more coherently for spraying her with paint. Wendy went as pink as her freckles.

I caught Lisa's eye. She winked. We both giggled. Was there something going on between Wendy and *Mr Speed*?

Wendy was all too happy to stay behind with me after school. We sometimes popped round other days too.

My mum and dad were thrilled that I'd made a new friend.

'Ask Lisa if she wants to come to tea,' said Mum.

So I did, though I was a bit worried about it. Sometimes kids are happy to be your friend at school but they don't want to be real tell-you-everything-come-to-my-sleepover friends with someone like me. But Lisa looked really pleased. So Wendy drove us both home in the special adapted car and Lisa met my mum and my dad and my big sister Lois. I felt a bit bothered because they all baby me a bit, especially my dad. He always fusses round me, chucking me under the chin, tickling me, treating me like a fairy princess.

'My dad's a bit daft,' I said with my voice machine, when Lisa and I were in my room.

'Your dad's *lovely*,' said Lisa. She looked strangely sad. But she smiled again as she peered all round my room. 'Your room's so fantastic, Natasha!'

My room would be the front room or dining room in most people's houses, but it's my bedroom because it's downstairs so it saves Mum or Dad hauling me up and down every day. I didn't want it all frilly and little girly. I've got deep navy carpet and curtains and a navy and white checked duvet and a white table the right height for my wheelchair and a big white bookshelf unit with loads of brightly jacketed books and white bowls containing my cactus collection. There's a big crystal mobile hanging near the windows so there are rainbow sparkles on the white walls whenever the sun shines.

'Oh, I had one little crystal hanging up where we used to live,' Lisa said, touching the mobile very gently with one finger. 'But someone broke it when we moved.'

'I know a shop where—' I started to say with my voice machine, but Lisa was shaking her head.

'No, I don't want another. It wouldn't be the same.' Her voice went wobbly. 'Nothing's the same any more.'

I didn't say, 'Tell me.' The voice machine would bark it out like a robot order. I just looked *'Tell me'* with my eyes. Lisa came and sat beside me and started telling me all this sad, sad, sad stuff about her dad and how he drinks all the time now and hits her mum. Lisa cried a little. I wished I could reach out properly and give her a cuddle. My arms went flailing wildly all over the place, but Lisa understood. She grabbed one of my hands and we held onto each other tightly.

I tried to think what it must be like to be Lisa. My dad has a can or two of lager when he watches football on the television but I've never seen him *drunk*. He did come back acting a bit silly after his office party. He came into my room to kiss me goodnight – but he was just funny-drunk, singing songs to me and pretending to tie my plaits into tangles.

I can't ever imagine Dad hitting anyone. He's never once smacked Lois or me, even if we were really naughty, and he'd *never* hit Mum. He teases her a little bit if she gets bossy but she just laughs. I don't think I could bear it if I had Lisa's dad.

I couldn't tell her all this on my laborious machine. I just held onto her hand and she squeezed it tight.

'You won't tell anyone, will you, Natasha?' she said without thinking.

'As if!' I said with my machine, and we both laughed a little shakily.

'Did you tell Mr Speed?'

'No! And I was going to type a bit of it on the Worry Website and then I couldn't. Hey, I saw you putting something on the website, Natasha. What did you put? Or is it private?'

'No. It was silly. The concert. I wanted to be in it. Like sing? Dance? Ha ha.'

'I'm not in it either. I didn't feel like it so I said I'd paint the scenery.'

'But you *could* be in it.' I couldn't say it with the right emphasis but she understood.

'Yes, I suppose I could be the all-singing ever-dancing Lisa and warble and twirl and sing . . . ?'

'*Don't worry, be happy!*'

Lisa laughed.

I said it again, hitting the 'worry' word on my keyboard several times to make it sound like a funny little chorus.

Lisa looked at me.

'Do that again.'

I did.

'And you can keep on doing that? It doesn't hurt your hand, does it?'

'No, but it hurts my *ears*,' I said. 'It sounds weird.'

'It sounds perfect! Natasha, we'll do a song together at the concert. We can make up the verses, something about Mr Speed's website – and then we can sing it. I'll do the verses and each chorus is . . . ?'

'Worry worry worry worry!'

That's just what we did! The concert was *soooo* cool. The fairy-tale pantomime was great and everyone admired the spectacular scenery. But it was the star turns that went down really well. Holly and her little sister did a dance together wearing wonderful embroidered new dresses – they looked so cute. Greg sang a song about falling in love. He might have meant it to  be serious but he kept rolling his eyes and clutching his heart and everyone got the giggles.

William and Samantha were the real surprise. I was getting nervous because it was nearly *our* turn and I so badly didn't want to let Lisa down. But I laughed so much at William mucking up his tricks and Samantha raising her eyebrows and tossing her hair and doing it for him that the tight feeling in my tummy disappeared. Everyone cheered and cheered William and Samantha. William's dad whistled and clapped like crazy and Samantha's dad was in tears. Samantha ran off the stage straight into his arms.

'Thank goodness *my* dad isn't here,' Lisa muttered to me. She had a little wave at her mum as she pushed me on stage.

Everyone went quiet and still. I knew they were all tense because of me. People who squirm around in wheelchairs don't usually perform on stage.

But once we got started it was OK. This is our *Worry Song*:

Worry worry worry worry
Worry worry worry worry
Have you got a worry
messing up your head?
Do you feel in a flurry?
Do you wish you were dead?

Worry worry worry worry
Worry worry worry worry
Do you have a secret fear?
Do you hate the way you look?
Do you shed a secret tear?
Seek an answer from a book?

Worry worry worry worry
Worry worry worry worry
Can't find a solution?
Can't get to sleep at night?
Do you worry about pollution,
starving people, men that fight?

Worry worry worry worry
Worry worry worry worry
Do your worries make you blush?
Are you scared to spit it out?
Do you blurt it in a rush?
Are you cast down in doubt?

Worry worry worry worry
Worry worry worry worry
Do you wet the bed?
Does your dad hit your mum?
Do you scream inside your head?
Does the pain make you numb?

Worry worry worry worry
Worry worry worry worry
Do you fuss about a spot?
Do you feel you are too fat?
Do you talk a lot of rot?
Do you feel a total prat?

Worry worry worry worry
Worry worry worry worry
Well, you know what to do
when your worries get you down.
The Worry Website's here for you
It will smooth out that frown.

Worry worry worry worry
Worry worry worry worry
Your friends will show they care
With comments frank but fond
It helps us all to share
And Mr Speed will wave his magic wand
To stop you going . . .
Worry worry worry worry
Worry worry worry worry
WORRY!

I said it was OK. It was more than OK. We were the glitter-girl stars of the show!

Mr Speed really does seem to be able to work magic because nearly everyone's worries have been sorted out. Even Mr Speed's. He sat hand in hand with Wendy throughout the entire concert!

ABOUT THE AUTHOR

JACQUELINE WILSON was born in Bath in 1945, but has
spent most of her life in Kingston-on-Thames, Surrey. She always wanted
to be a writer and wrote her first 'novel' when she was nine, filling count-
less Woolworths' exercise books as she grew up. She started work at a pub-
lishing company and then went on to work as a journalist on *Jackie* maga-
zine (which was named after her) before turning to writing fiction full-time.

Since 1990 Jacqueline has written prolifically for children and
been awarded many of the UK's top awards for children's books, including
the Smarties Prize in 2000 and the Guardian Children's Fiction Award and
the Children's Book of the Year in 1999. Jacqueline was awarded an OBE in
the Queen's Birthday Honours list, in Golden Jubilee Year, 2002.

Over 9 million copies of Jacqueline's books have now been
sold in the UK and approximately 50,000 copies of her books are sold each
month. An avid reader herself, Jacqueline has a personal collection of more
than 15,000 books.

She lives in Surrey and has one grown-up daughter.

'A brilliant young writer of wit and subtlety whose stories are never
patronising and are often complex and many-layered'
The Times

'Jacqueline Wilson has a rare gift for writing lightly and
amusingly about emotional issues'
Bookseller

'Wilson writes like a child, and children instantly recognize
themselves in her characters. The tone of voice is faultless,
her stories are about the problems many children face, and her
plots work with classic simplicity... a subtle art is concealed by
artlessness, and some might call that genius'
Daily Telegraph